ABOVE THE FIRE

ABOVE THE FIRE

MICHAEL O'DONNELL

BLACK
STONE
PUBLISHING

Printed in the United States of America

First edition: 2023
ISBN 979-8-200-98775-7
Fiction / General

Version 1

Blackstone Publishing
31 Mistletoe Rd.
Ashland, OR 97520

www.BlackstonePublishing.com

for James

It was impossible to convey what it feels like up there to those who have stayed below.

—Paolo Cognetti,
THE EIGHT MOUNTAINS

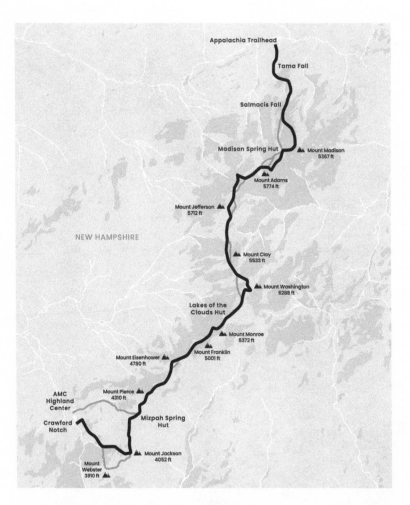

PRESIDENTIAL TRAVERSE
—UNITED STATES—

DISTANCE
23 miles / 37 km

HIGHEST POINT
6288 ft / 1917 m
(Mount Washington)

TOTAL ALTITUDE
9000 ft / 2743 m

TIME TO FINISH
Typically 2 to 4 days

ONE

The boy and his father broke through the tree line and felt the sun on their faces. Rocks that had been in shadow were replaced by others warm to the touch. They paused to catch their breath and take in the view. The last few sections of trail had been steep, but the boy had refused to stop and rest. He seemed determined to display his strength and outpace his companion. Now he relented at last. They drank water. Standing on a blade-shaped promontory made of shale, they gazed silently in all directions. The sound of their breathing competed only with an occasional gust of wind. Golden afternoon light illuminated a dozen peaks as well as the valley to the east. Thousands of trees filled the space below them under a vast expanse of sky. The man placed a hand on his son's shoulder. Such was their relative height that this seemed to be the hand's natural resting place.

Before them the trail descended to a small cluster of structures, which lay sheltered in a hollow upon the saddle between two peaks. The main cabin had the size and proportions of a house. A planked deck surrounded it on three sides. Behind it, on pallets, rested two large plastic tanks for storing water. Another smaller hut stood adjacent. At a distance of twenty yards was a platform where four slender wooden stalls had been erected at the edge of a small rock face. If this was like the previous night's cabin, the man knew, these would be the outhouses. An all-terrain vehicle stood idle beneath a crude lean-to shelter. In between these various structures, among the rocks and boulders and beneath prayer flags strung above, were several picnic tables where the bright garments of other backpackers stood out against the mild colors of the earth.

They picked their way down into the camp. As they hiked into the alpine bowl, the wind disappeared altogether, and the sound of their walking poles against the rocks made a loud report. Scrubby brush and stunted greenery, accented by yellow wildflowers, lined the trail on either side. Crude timber walkways crossed over parts of the path that had grown muddy from frequent use. The damp wood lay soft and pockmarked, flexing underfoot. As they approached the camp, another hiker passed, going the other direction. She wore a tasseled beanie and carried a heavy pack meant to last for weeks, its steel frame hard as the bed of a truck. Climbing the day's final few steps, the boy and his father discarded their own packs against the deck with a sigh. Then they removed their boots and entered the hut, their shoulders bunched and weary from the long march.

The hut warden was a thin, bearded man with gray hair and glasses. He wore wool socks under camp sandals and assumed the reflective nature of a monk. As they entered, he sat upon his stool unmoving like some timeless sentinel of the forest. After confirming their reservation and prepayment, he gave a tour of the Madison Spring Hut campus, walking with his hands clasped lightly behind his back and carrying himself at his own remove. Smiling often but saying little, he gave an air of benevolent rigidity as he recited the house rules in his hoarse tenor. He showed the main cabin, where boots were forbidden; the dormitory rooms, where they were free to choose any top and bottom bunk; the fireplace, which must be stocked daily with fuel from the chopping block; the kitchen, with its detailed protocols for conserving water and packing out waste; the solar panel, which provided a small daily charge for the exclusive benefit of the staff; and the outhouses, with their ingenious gravity-based water can for hand-washing after use of the privy. Fixing them with a stern and humorless eye, the warden said: "Please keep the toilet lids closed. We have a woodchuck problem."

After their tour, the warden, whose name was David, invited them to a complimentary hot beverage as well as a cookie. Going forward, he said, refreshments cost twenty-five cents, paid by an honor system. The man prepared himself tea and made a cocoa for his son. They each picked up a snickerdoodle. Baking these confections in the kitchen's small gas oven comprised the simple labor of David's afternoons. The main room of the cabin was an open-planned space with five tables set perpendicularly against the exterior wall. The interior wall divided the great room from the kitchen. At the far end, away from the door, was a fireplace upon a hearth of flagstones and surrounded by camp chairs. Drying clothing—long johns and thick socks, damp from the elements—hung above it on lines. In the kitchen stood two plastic basins and two double gas ranges, as well as cupboards and bins. Mugs and plates lay facedown on steel racks. Although the facility lacked ready electricity or plumbing, various systems were set in place for fresh water to be brought up from the river and used for boiling and cooking. Non-potable water allowed for the washing of dishes and was discarded into buckets.

The boy waited for his father to lead them to a place to sit. He grew shy in the presence of the other hikers, even on their second night in such a cabin. Several tables were occupied by young adults. One group was deep in a card game; another had a bottle of wine and laughed occasionally among themselves. The man led his son to an empty table and set down their things to eat. The room was bright and cheerful, ringed with windows and outfitted in blond cedar. It was much better than the previous night's hut at Carter Notch. The boy unselfconsciously sat next to his father rather than across from him. His feet did not touch the ground, and his knees were the thickest parts of his legs. He would turn eight years old in the spring. This was his first hiking trip. He asked the man to taste his cocoa first to gauge its temperature. Together they sipped their drinks and watched the sun set over the mountains.

✳✳✳

They selected their bunks carefully. The boy wanted to be near the dormitory room's windows. His father said it would be colder there and that the sunlight would wake them early. But that part of the room was not as dark in the gloaming, and this was the boy's chief consideration. The boy took the top bunk, and his father placed his own pack below. He made his son's bed first, unrolling the sleeping bag and cotton liner, inflating the camp pillow, putting Aaron the stuffed aardvark next to it, then setting out the headlamp, toiletries, and pajamas. After he finished and began work on his own bunk, his son climbed up the ladder and began to play with his spaceship toy, making soft sounds to mimic its flight and voicing the different characters that consumed his imagination.

The spaceship had been a subject of contention as they packed for the trip. It was fragile, made of hundreds of tiny bricks. "It will break during the hike," the man said. "Spaceships don't work very well in backpacks."

"But I want to bring it," his son replied obstinately. "Maybe we can reinforce the wings."

"OK, but if it breaks, promise you won't be too upset?"

"We can rebuild it if it breaks."

"We can always try."

The boy's face had burst into a grin. All he heard was the news that he could bring his toy. "Promise!" he cried, skipping away before his victory could be diminished. They had reinforced the wings from underneath with bricks of a complementary color and removed several of the superficial parts most liable to snap off. Since then, the boy had devised a careful system for storing the spaceship in the top panel of his backpack, wrapped in his stocking cap and cushioned by extra pairs of socks. He checked on it frequently.

As dinnertime approached a familiar tension settled in between them. The boy wanted them to eat alone, apart from others, while his father said they must be sociable and try to make friends. The boy did not like being viewed as a novelty, the youngest person on the trail or in a hut. He was always questioned about his endurance, whether he liked school, and whether he missed his mother. The conversations all seemed to end with a laugh at his expense as the adults wished they had as much youth and resilience. He did not yet understand the good nature of this conviviality. Meeting people and forming brief but strong friendships were two of the things his father enjoyed most about journeys to the mountains. The man was not a naturally gregarious person but had found that other hikers and backpackers were often of a like mind and in a mood to socialize. They were doing what they loved best, and this enterprise, coupled with the beautiful surroundings, predisposed them to connect. The man knew that he needed more such opportunities.

"Fine, but can we at least not sit with that guy in the orange socks?" his son said irritably. "He smells and he talks about snakes all the time." They had been buttonholed by an awkward solo hiker the previous evening. Neither of them had enjoyed his company.

"We'll try to sit with someone else," his father said.

As they entered the common room, he quickly scanned the tables. He saw several familiar faces from the previous cabin, but no one the boy would want to sit with again. There was a new family of four. Something in the parents' open expressions reminded him of the strong plain chords of folk music. They worked together chopping vegetables on a small cutting board. He walked over and asked if they could sit down. They were friendly and said of course. Their two children, a boy and a girl, looked to be young teenagers and kept to themselves in the inner corner of the table by the windows. The man and his son set down their water bottles and then prepared their dehydrated meals using hot water that was kept near-boiling for the common use of the travelers. As they sat waiting for their meals to cook in the dehydrated bags, the man struck up a conversation.

"And what are you making?"

"Couscous," the woman answered pleasantly. "With carrots, onions, cashews, and raisins. You see?" She showed the finished chopping as her husband stirred. Their daughter was carefully putting the leftover vegetable waste into a small plastic bag.

"It looks tasty," the man said. "We should be more ambitious: we just eat these dehydrated meals."

"Ah, those are very nice," she replied. "But so expensive."

"And, actually, not that nice," the man said good-naturedly. They all laughed. "I'm Doug. This is my son, Tim."

"How do you do. I'm Linda. My husband, Ove." They introduced their children as well. Ove was fair and had handsome features. The sun had bleached the edges of his hair. His face had an honest look. He wore a white bandana loosely around his throat, and the crow's feet at the corners of his eyes carried dust from the day's hike. Linda bore an expression of mischief and mirth. She looked like she would be the first to accept a challenge or a dare: to plunge into an ice-cold lake, or to run at full speed through a dark field. The couple were at ease with each other and their children. Doug liked them both.

"Where are you from?" he asked. Tim looked on quietly, listening.

"Copenhagen. And you?"

"So far away! We're from near Boston, just a few hours from here. How are you enjoying New Hampshire?"

"Oh, it is beautiful here, very beautiful," said Ove, who took over the conversation as his wife helped their children. "I have always wanted to see the White Mountains."

"You're on holiday?"

"Yes," said Ove. "We've been here two weeks. A bit of sight-seeing, now some backpacking. Next we go to Chicago."

"Have you been to the States before?"

"I have been here for business, but for my family it is the first time," Ove said.

"Where did you do your sightseeing?" Doug asked.

"We were in Boston, and New York, of course."

"New York, New York."

Ove laughed. "It was overwhelming. The children could not believe it. We stayed two days, but after that, I think, it was time for us to move on."

"And Chicago—will you fly there?"

"We will fly there," Ove said, accepting the prompt. His English was fluent but charmingly accented. "I have not been to Chicago before." He turned to Tim and said in a kind but not patronizing way, "Tim, what was your favorite part of to-day's hike?"

Tim looked shyly at his father, at a loss for how to answer. Then he seemed to respond to something in Ove's manner and found his confidence. "The hawk!" he said with a smile.

"You saw a hawk?" asked Ove.

"A goshawk. They're very rare."

"We enjoy birds," said Doug.

"Was it hunting?" Ove asked Tim.

"It was circling very high," said Tim. "That means it was looking for prey. Probably a smaller bird."

"Did it dive?"

"No, it just circled over and over again. We watched it for a long time."

"Hawks have very good eyes," said Ove in a serious tone. "That's how they can see from so high. You must have good eyes as well, Tim. To have spotted such a rare bird today."

Tim made the small, contained half smile he sometimes displayed when he felt proud and was trying not to show it. Doug saw this expression just once or twice a year.

***

After the meal, they lingered long enough to enjoy conversation with their new friends and then withdrew to sit by the fire. Tim drank another cocoa while Doug sipped whiskey from a flask. The flask had belonged to his own father and was wrapped in time-creased leather. The leather smelled of bourbon even when the flask was empty. The fire made for cheerful viewing, and they gazed into it silently, listening to the crackle and hiss. Outside, the temperature had plummeted in the October chill. The fire warmed their legs and singed their stockinged toes. "I wish we had marshmallows," said Tim.

Candlelight adorned the tables as a blue twilight enveloped the warm room. The smell of cedar and pine needles combined to produce an intoxicating alpine essence. Some of the guests chatted quietly while others played checkers or chess. The man in the orange socks read a paperback novel. David sat on his stool and occasionally recorded a thought in the journal he kept at hand, using a pencil that had been worn down to the nub. He responded pleasantly to anyone who addressed him but never initiated conversations of his own.

"He doesn't say much," said Tim.

"I think he spends a lot of time by himself," replied Doug.

"Do you think he built the fire?"

"I think he probably did."

"I wonder if he used lint from a dryer." Doug had shown Tim how to use lint as a lightweight fire starter while camping.

"Maybe," he said. "I'll bet he's really good at building fires."

Tim sighed loudly in his inscrutable way. "Yeah. I'll bet." At one time Doug would have interpreted a sigh like this to mean his son was homesick, or not enjoying himself, or sad in some existential sense. But he had come to know him well enough to understand it was a simpler care. He probably just wished he had some lint. Or that he had gotten to start the fire.

"Let's walk around outside a bit and see how cold it is before we go to bed," he suggested to the boy.

"So it feels cozy in our sleeping bags?"

"So it feels cozy."

They slipped out of their camp shoes and into their hiking boots without tying the laces. It was much colder than when they had arrived, although the wind had died. A few stars were beginning to emerge overhead. They looked west, where the last light of the day showed the silhouettes of several peaks. The light created a sort of darkening rainbow up from the horizon, with colors from pale blue through indigo to black overhead.

They made their preparations for bed, brushing their teeth and saving the final trip to the outhouses for last. When it came time to change into pajamas, the boy raised his arms above his head and his father helped him out of his shirt. They sat in the top bunk and together by headlamp read *The Hobbit*, with its stories of wizards and dragons that captured Tim's imagination. The book dragged in some places, and Doug was obliged to skip ahead or risk losing his son's attention. Some evenings

Tim grew manic at bedtime, using any excuse at hand to ward off the inevitable. On other nights, such as this one, he became contemplative beyond his years and wanted to converse rather than read. The dynamic between them could shift unexpectedly and was as fragile as the interaction between man and animal. Sometimes Tim seemed to spoil for a fight, becoming argumentative and causing his father to parry rather than engage. Other times he would be as sweet as a seven-year-old could be.

"How long have these mountains been here?" he asked his father.

"Millions of years."

"How did they get here?"

"The Earth slowly moved, and when parts of it collided together it pushed upward, forming them."

"How long did that take?"

"Millions of years."

"How do you know?"

"I read about it."

"In the newspaper?"

"No, in a book."

"What was it called?"

Doug yawned. "I can't remember."

"Could I read that book?"

"Sure."

"You still have it?"

"I think so."

"But how will you find it, if you don't remember what it's called?" Tim was always looking for chinks in the armor of his father's logic.

"I remember what it looks like."

"What color is it?"

"Blue."

Tim said nothing for a few moments. Then: "Dad? Are these your favorite mountains?"

"Yes, they're my favorites."

"Why?"

"Because I used to come here with Mom."

"Did she like it here?"

Doug paused. "Well, she never liked the mountains quite as much as me. But she did like the view."

"Same as us."

"Same as us."

"Goodnight, Dad."

"Goodnight, my sweet boy."

***

He woke in the space between light and dream as a wan mountain sun filtered in through the window. It caught the blond curls of his hair and his pale blue eyes. The lines on his forehead and in his cheeks had deepened in his forty-first year. He shifted in his sleeping bag, and the sound of his limbs against the nylon made a loud rustle in the silent dormitory. She was not next to him. His waking mind still took a moment to remember. He heard his son's steady breathing in the bunk above and knew that he was still asleep. After climbing out of his sleeping bag, he checked that the boy was safely away from the edge of his high bunk and pulled on his fleece against the cold of the mountain cabin.

In the main room, David had already heated water and

was sipping tea in a unique mug that looked to be of Japanese provenance. Doug nodded to him and prepared coffee using his travel filter. No one else was about. He sat and opened the leather-bound journal he brought with him everywhere and had received as a gift long ago. Its epigraph was a quotation from Karen Blixen: "The cure for anything is salt water: sweat, tears, or the sea." Sipping and reflecting on the day before and the day ahead, he filled it with his thoughts as he watched the sunrise in the east. The weather was clear and fine.

Writing in the journal was a ritual that had replaced the morning newspaper during a challenging time in his life. It had been a difficult period for the country, and the news was relentlessly grim day after day. He found that staring at each morning's headlines before his mind even cleared fully from sleep set him on a path to dourness, fixing lines at the corners of his mouth and a stoop in his shoulders. He began to think, in the seconds between waking and rising, what will it be today? How many dead or what new scandal or what piece of environmental hopelessness will they write about? So he began leaving the newspaper on the curb and collecting it later, when he felt up to it. He started his day instead by writing. He would write about work, or friends who caused him to worry. An evening at a restaurant with his wife. Sometimes the journal became something more like a commonplace book, filled with clippings and scraps, photographs, and lists. It contained his reflections on the books he had read and the movies he had seen. But mostly he wrote about his son. How he had grown and what he had said and done. What type of child he was, and what type of young man he was becoming.

Doug took out his pen and wrote: *"T was strong on the*

trail yesterday. He complained far less than the day before and I had to persuade him to stop for lunch. The water straw helped now that it is finally working; he can take small sips throughout the day instead of stopping, removing the pack, and getting out his water bottle for a drink. So I think he was better hydrated. Also, this gave him fewer opportunities to complain. He made a very determined push to the high point of the trail shortly before we reached the cabin. I think he is enjoying the trip so far. I want him to like the mountains as much as I do. Silly projection, but there it is. He is still very moody. 80% of the time he is a delightful and charming boy, and much of that time he is downright exuberant. But then it's like a switch will throw and he's suddenly sullen, or aggressive, or despairing. I can watch it happen, without any rhyme or reason. Often it occurs in the early afternoon, and I suspect has something to do with digesting his lunch. But yesterday it was late morning when he clearly wanted to pick a fight for no good reason, over the slightest pretext. When I wouldn't engage, he became hopeless and insisted nothing would work: we wouldn't find the cabin, we would run out of food, we would get lost in the forest. All nonsensical things. I don't like bickering and don't think he's observed this behavior in me. Where does it come from? What do I do with it?"

Doug set down his pen and sipped his coffee. There was a time when he had censored what he wrote in the journal in the event someone would one day read it. But he had come to realize that its only usefulness lay in candor. It had to be a mirror to his honest thoughts, or it would become a pointless exercise in mental gymnastics and rationalization. He turned back to it and made several observations about the weather, their lodgings for the night, and the topography of their hike before closing the journal on his pen. He prepared oatmeal with walnuts for his breakfast and ate it slowly, gazing out the window.

"Looking for the *Himmelbjerget*?"

He started out of his reverie to see Linda setting her things down at the far side of his table. Her hair was wild, and she wore a fleece two sizes too big—likely Ove's.

"Sorry, the what?"

"Sky mountain," she said, sitting down. "It's the highest point in Denmark, although actually not very high, only about 150 meters. People gather there in my country. There is a famous tower on it in honor of King Frederik."

"You'll have to remind me when he reigned."

"Oh, 1830s, 1840s. He gave us our constitution."

"Have you been to the sky mountain?"

She smiled winningly. "That is where Ove and I met, as students. We were both traveling. So little to climb in Denmark, you know, such a flat country." She studied him for a moment. "You are married also?"

"I was."

"Ah, divorced."

Doug looked down at the table for a moment. "My wife passed away several years ago. Tim's mother. She used to love to come to the mountains. She would be here right now, but . . ." He looked up, unsure what to say. "So it's me and Tim this time."

Linda looked at him kindly. "Sorry," she said with a tender smile. "And now you come with your boy. He is good hiker, like his mother."

Doug smiled. "It's his first time. I hiked this trail twenty years ago. I've been waiting to share the mountains with him. Hopefully it's not too soon."

"My advice is, when he says he wants to finish, then finish—don't push him too far the first time." She changed the topic cheerfully. "Oatmeal for breakfast, so?"

"Oatmeal and walnuts. I forgot to pack brown sugar. What it really needs is some chocolate."

Her eye glinted. "I *always* have chocolate. I go hiking and my favorite thing, Ove says, is I eat whatever I want. And I do, ha ha!" With that, she placed a thick bar of chocolate on the table within his reach and got up to prepare her own breakfast as she whistled with a fine vibrato.

***

Before Doug and Tim set off for their day's hike, Doug learned from Ove that his family was going the same direction and was making for the same cabin. They arranged for the two families to have dinner together. As they spoke, they noticed David placing bags and a small gasoline canister on the ATV parked nearby.

"I wonder if he's making a supply run?" said Doug.

"Maybe going up to the top to sit and meditate," said Ove, grinning.

"Maybe." Doug laughed. He looked up to the sky. "Going to be colder today."

"Yes, we may need our puffies."

Doug looked at the sky once more and prepared to set off. "Good hike, safe journey," he said, shaking hands. "See you for dinner."

Tim occasionally liked to assert his independence by setting the pace and keeping twenty or thirty feet between himself and his father, stealing furtive glances back. He did so as they set out on the third day of their trek. Whenever the trail was unclear, he would wait for his father to catch up and then, after receiving instruction, hurry ahead once more to regain his buffer. The path wound up and over the saddle and back into the face of the wind. The next peak before them was Mount Adams, and they hiked around its shoulder. Then the trail proceeded south in a gradual descent over scree and loose dirt into waist-high evergreens and scrubby brush. The trail took them from peak to peak throughout the Presidential Range, keeping them at or above the tree line. Often it cut steeply upward for several hundred meters to allow a summit of another peak. Nine summits comprised the Presidential Traverse, with the highest, Mount Washington, at the center. They wore long sleeves and waterproof jackets to cut the wind, as well as gloves. Their wool hats came on and off as exertion and wind required. Tim would lean his shoulder into hard gusts when they came every few minutes. His small frame seemed liable to fly away in too hard a blow.

As they walked and established a pace, Doug felt the stiffness begin to work out of his legs. He was lean and strong, standing just under six feet and carrying broad shoulders that nevertheless ached for the first hours of every morning. A knot in one of his calves began to loosen as he raised his face to the mountain air, which passed over his cheeks and lips. His breathing took on a rhythm and his mind began to clear. This would be the work of the day. Boots on a trail, inching their way forward, out of doors and out of mind except where he let his thoughts wander. They would do one thing at a time: make a fire, drink cold water, doze in the shade. All the while the clarifying beat of their stride would lend purpose to the exertion. They were proceeding a span of twelve miles, from one shelter to another, spurred on by the reward of a meal with new friends, time spent together, and the simple accomplishment of a goal. Their business was as ancient as footprints and as simple as onrushing wind. They were free.

They had seen little wildlife so far in their hike, aside from squirrels and beaver, and of course the hawk that had captivated them both. Black bears were not uncommon in this country, and Doug kept his eyes open. Tim was out front on his own. Doug didn't go so far as to tap his poles together rhythmically or call aloud at intervals as he tended to do against the threat of grizzlies in the western mountains. Black bears were furtive and not known to be aggressive unless their young were disturbed. At any rate, Tim would never have countenanced such measures. He had recently begun to show signs of self-awareness and embarrassment of his parent. At a recent stop to an ice-cream truck, Doug had struggled to understand his son's order and then dropped a five-dollar bill. The boy had actually slapped his palm to his forehead in mortification. As though the ice-cream man were some celebrity smirking at a child's discomfiture. The cost of the spontaneous treat was suddenly far too high, and Tim ate his popsicle with little interest. Doug knew that there was nothing but to let such moods pass. To lower a line and attempt to pull his son out was only to be pulled in himself. The new phase of embarrassment was harmless enough, but it prefigured the closing of an innocent era, when they might hold hands freely or sing aloud together. Always he was growing. His father sighed and set about producing a steady soundtrack of footfalls, poles on rocks, and throat clearings so that any animals would hear them and move well out of their way.

He had not realized until meeting the Danish family how singular an experience it was, to keep company exclusively with a seven-year-old child. Aside from a few casual attempts at conversation in the prior hut and on the trail, he had spent the past few days interacting with no one other than his young son. To do so successfully, he had to discard many of the niceties and customs that had become second nature in his adult life. As a rule, he did not correct others. He disliked pedantry and often felt that who was right or wrong about a thing mattered less than the equilibrium and dynamic at play between people. But he had learned that, with a child, a failure to correct could lead to misunderstanding and friction of its own. On the first morning of the hike, Tim had placed one of his backpack straps backward and asked if it was right. It was an exasperated moment already because of a poor night's sleep and a harried start. To keep things on an even keel Doug had said, "It's fine." When Tim realized after seeing himself in a reflection later in the day that the strap was in fact misplaced, he felt hurt and betrayed by his father's false advice. He sulked for a half hour afterward. His expression for the rest of the day revealed his lingering mistrust.

The father and son also had difficulty communicating because of a gap in literal-mindedness. Doug would skip several steps ahead of a question to the implications of its answer, frustrating the boy. Tim had recently asked how much longer until lunch. Instead of answering, Doug had said, "I told you, you should have eaten a bigger breakfast." But Tim had not said: "I am hungry." Instead, he had asked for information: "When is lunch?" He did not know when his next meal would arrive and had no way of finding out other than from his parent. He could have had many different reasons for wanting to know. But his father didn't provide the information and instead made a criticism that assumed something about the question. Something that in fact wasn't there: the boy had been thinking about the next break from his backpack, not mourning an empty stomach that he had neglected to fill. It was as though the two of them spoke a different dialect of the same language. Unlearning these conventions of adult interaction took imagination, as well as a wellspring of patience.

They watered at a cluster of boulders where the trail bent around on itself in a pair of switchbacks. For this first break in the day's hike, they did not take off their backpacks. They were harder to put back on than they were worth removing. All of the heavy equipment was in Doug's bag, but Tim's was still full and bulky for his fifty-pound body. At the end of each day, his knees ached, and on the first night it had caused him to cry. Doug had administered children's Tylenol but had mistakenly brought the grape flavor that the boy disliked intensely. Leaning against the boulders, they sipped water and shared a candy bar.

"How are the knees?"

"OK."

"Not too sore?"

"Nope."

"You're setting a good pace out front. What have you seen?"

"Oh, you know—same stuff as you, I guess."

"I liked the waterfall."

"Me too. Do you think there were fish in it?"

"Probably."

"What happens to fish when they go down a waterfall?"

"They must hold their breath."

They looked at each other for a moment and then burst out laughing. Whatever tension had inexplicably existed was suddenly gone.

"Dad?"

"Yes, buddy?"

"Where was that family from? The one we ate dinner with?"

"They're from a country called Denmark. It's in Europe."

"Which one is Europe?"

"It's the one right above Africa. On the right-hand page. The yellow one."

"Have you been there?"

"I've been to Europe. But I haven't been to Denmark. I'd like to go sometime."

"Do they have mountains?"

"Not really. The mom told me that they have one really big hill but not many mountains."

"Do you think our mom would have liked their mom?"

"I think they would have been friends."

"Did our mom have a lot of friends?"

"Yes, she did. She made friends easily."

"Sometimes it's hard for me to make friends."

"You know, me too."

"If Mom was here, she could teach us."

"I would like that."

"How did Mom make friends?"

"I think Mom was a very good listener. People like to be listened to."

"She *was* a good listener."

"Mom would be proud of us for making some new friends on our trip. We're going to see them at dinner tonight. Their mom said you were a good hiker."

"I like their mom. She's nice. Her teeth are very straight."

"Yes, I suppose they are."

"Maybe we could go there sometime. To Denmark. The two of us."

"I'd like that."

Tim sighed. "I guess we should keep going. Let's walk together for a while."

***

They encountered several others on the trail during the morning. A Cub Scout group and their den leader were making slow progress. They were bogged down by too much gear and frequent stopping. The adult looked harried from childcare responsibilities. Later, a pair of young runners blazed by, causing Doug and Tim to practically leap off the path. They shouted thanks behind them without slowing. They wore shorts and tank tops and carried nothing but a water bottle each.

"They were going so fast!" Tim said excitedly.

"Yeah, they must be in really good shape. They're called trail runners: people who go running in the mountains."

"When I grow up, I want to be a trail runner."

"You'd be a good one."

"Did you ever want to be a trail runner?"

"You know, I didn't. I like going running, and I like the mountains. But I always felt like it's a little too dangerous. If anything were to happen, those guys don't even have jackets."

"What do you mean, 'If anything were to happen?'"

"Well, suppose one of them sprained his ankle."

"Then his friend could go get help."

"That's true. But maybe it takes him a few hours to get to help and a few hours for the help to get back to him. And say a storm blows in while he's waiting with his sprained ankle, wearing shorts. It starts to rain—or worse, it starts to snow. It can get pretty cold quickly up here in the mountains. Suddenly he's in bad trouble."

Tim thought for a moment. "He could build a shelter!"

Doug smiled. "Very clever, yes. That's probably a good idea. But that's one of the tough things about trail running. You don't carry much with you. No tools. Nothing to build a shelter with."

"He could find a cave."

"Another good idea. Although that could make it hard for his friend to find him later, if the cave isn't nearby."

"I guess it's complicated, huh."

"Afraid so. It's complicated."

After lunch they found a comfortable glade and decided to nap. Doug made a pillow of Tim's backpack and stretched out on a bed of dry pine needles, reaching out his arm to provide a place for his son's head to lay. They were still for several moments before the boy began to squirm restlessly. He kept his eyes closed in a pantomime of sleep, but his movements betrayed him. After a few minutes more he stood and said, "I'm going to explore." Doug told him to stay where he could see him, and to be careful. He closed his eyes once again and dropped off into a dreamless doze, borne away from consciousness by the sound of wind rustling through grass.

When he woke, an hour had passed. He fought off an immediate urge to panic when his son was not within reach or view. Instead, he forced himself to breathe in the alpine air that they had sought out together and to luxuriate in his mountain rest. This was a safe place. The boy would not stray far. He was inquisitive but sensible, and above all, tentative even at a few steps' remove from his parent. Doug lay still and listened. Wind and open space. Intermittent birdsong. Soon enough he heard a high sweet voice and knew that he needn't have worried. The boy was singing "Jingle Bells."

Walking over, Doug saw that his son had found a small, cozy space for himself in the crotch of two fallen trees. There were several sticks littered around, as well as an empty wrapper of Goldfish crackers and Doug's phone.

"Hi, Dad," he said cheerfully. "Did you have a good nap?"

"Hey, buddy. Sure did. What you been doing?"

"Nothing. I found this cool fort. These are my swords. And I took a bunch of pictures on your phone. Want to see?"

"Sure. Show me." Doug sat down on a fallen log and traced with his eye the delicate lines between neck and ear, eye and nose, of the boy in profile as he navigated through the phone's controls. Tim's small fingers were deft on the screen, much better suited to the task than his own.

"This one shows a chipmunk that was running around. He's blurry."

"I see him."

"Here's you napping."

"Was I snoring?"

Tim laughed without looking up. "A little bit. These are some pictures of my shoes"—swiping by the outtakes with good-natured impatience—"and here is a river down there that I saw. You can see it if you zoom."

"What a photographer you are. And you were about to clean up your wrapper before it blows away?"

Tim smiled as he looked for other pictures to showcase. "I was just about to," he said, in no great hurry.

***

That evening's cabin was situated in a less spectacular position, several hundred feet below the tree line and with no vista in any direction. The area was heavily forested, and they had to descend steeply before arriving, closely watching the signposts at trail junctions. The cabin itself was a tall A-frame structure that rose to a height of three stories and was built of darkened pine. Shingles formed its roof and overhung the stone walls. There was a feeling of claustrophobia in the small surrounding clearing. The mountain rose steeply upslope and fell away to the south, all under an evergreen canopy. The air was protected from wind but nevertheless cool and damp. For the first time since they had gained the tree line several days earlier, they encountered mosquitoes. They both hurried to get inside.

Two twenty-somethings supervised the cabin. Its entryway opened onto a great room that conveyed more air and space than the previous night's lodging while offering less cheer. The windows, hemmed in by pine trees, gave little light. Wooden beams crossed the high vaulted ceiling and dangled circular electric lamps, but these cast only a dim gloom into corners. There were more tables, as though this cabin could accommodate a larger number of travelers. Detritus from a prior meal dotted several of them, with crumbs and the rings left behind from mugs littering a table. Apparently, they kept house less fastidiously here at Mizpah Spring than in the Madison Spring Hut. The map laminated by the door revealed that they were within six miles of a trailhead with a parking lot that some day-hikers used as their launching point. There may have been a higher volume of casual travelers here. The cabin also stood at a key junction of the Appalachian Trail. Long-distance through-hikers used the space for resupply, mail, and emergency shelter.

The young man who checked them in seemed as resigned to his task as the desk worker of an airport hotel. At first, he could not find their reservation and seemed ready to turn them away, no matter that one of them was a child near tears at the thought. Doug kept his voice steady through anger, and soon sorted out the mistake. The bunk rooms, accessed through dark hallways, were slightly less gloomy, and they selected their spaces. Tim nevertheless disliked the new cabin. Between its unfamiliar surroundings and darker atmosphere, not to mention the difficult check-in and the fatigue of the day, he seemed tentative and small.

"Could you ask if they have cookies?"

"Sure, buddy, I'll ask. Just give me a minute to finish making this bed. We'll be glad to have them made later."

"OK, but do you think you'll be done soon? I'm hungry."

Doug put aside the linens and made himself see things through the boy's eyes. "You're right. I could use a snack too. Let's go see."

There were recently baked brownies cut in thick wedges on a platter near the kitchen. Doug rummaged for change, but the young woman in charge saw the excitement in Tim's eyes and waved away payment with a smile. She bent over the platter and put her hands on her knees, addressing the boy in the terms of a serious matter.

"OK. So. This side has walnuts. This side has chocolate chips. What do you think?"

Tim smiled in delight and looked up at his father for an indication of how to proceed.

"Your pick, my guy. I know what I'm getting."

"Walnuts?"

"You guessed it."

"I'll get chocolate chips." He studied the options carefully and selected the most advantageous brownie, symmetrical and unburnt. They carried their snacks over to a table and sat down. The young woman brought over a glass of milk and winked at Tim.

"What do you say?" Doug asked.

"Thank you," Tim said, washing down his first bite.

Later, as they waited for their Danish friends and anticipated dinner together, Doug wrote in his journal, and Tim took his father's suggestion to write a letter to his cousin. In his rushed handwriting, refusing to be prompted on what to say, he wrote: "*Dear Justin, How are you? My dad and I are on a hiking trip. We saw a hawk. Who is your favorite Batman villain? Mine is Two Face. I'm going to ask for a trampoline for my birthday. Write back. Love, Tim.*" Underneath this, he drew a picture of a mountain cabin with smoke curling from the chimney.

"I think it's very nice," his father said.

The door opened and a hiker strode in, not stopping to remove his boots. He began speaking animatedly with the young man at check-in. Doug watched but could not hear them. They seemed to be discussing something that had happened out on the trail.

"You keep coloring," he said to Tim, who had not noticed. He kept his voice light. "I'm going to go see if this guy has seen our friends, so we know how much longer we have to wait until dinner."

"OK," said Tim, not looking up from his work.

Doug walked over and began to listen as the hiker spoke quickly, in a low voice.

". . . and for both of you to stay put. We need one of you

available on the radio at all times for the next twelve hours, so you'll have to take turns—"

"What, like overnight?" asked the desk worker.

"Yes, overnight too," said the hiker impatiently. "How many guests do you have on the roster for tonight?"

"Let me look here . . . thirteen. Six have checked in so far, we've got a few singles, a few couples, and a family of four on the way."

"And how many check out tomorrow?"

The desk worker again looked through his papers. "Looks like ten are heading out in the morning."

"Any locals?"

"Nobody even from New Hampshire."

Doug interjected. "Sorry, is something wrong?"

The hiker looked up at him, startled. He appeared to be in his early fifties and a seasoned outdoorsman. His face was weather-beaten and lightly stubbled a blondish-gray color. Doug noticed that he wore high-quality gear that had seen many seasons but was in good repair. The sleeves of his technical shirt were pushed up his forearms and he wore a large circular digital watch with an altimeter readout. His boots were well-used and made from durable leather that could last a lifetime. He looked at Doug and seemed to weigh what to do next. "I'd better make an announcement."

"Announce what? Is someone injured? We have friends out on the trail."

The hiker hesitated and looked at the desk worker.

"Listen," said Doug, keeping his voice low. "I've got a seven-year-old sitting over there. I don't want you to scare him. Tell me what's going on, and he and I might step outside while you speak to the group."

The hiker looked hard at Doug. "You're right. OK. I don't know quite how to explain this." He paused to take a breath. "Something's going on down below. We're not sure what. We've lost communications with everyone who's not on our closed mountain network. Phones, internet, broadband—it's all down. We can still reach ranger stations in the national forest on CB radio, but nothing hooked into Wi-Fi or landlines."

"So your network crashed? That doesn't seem like such a big deal. Why all the fuss?"

"No, that's not it. We sometimes have problems with our system, but this is different. Nobody's personal cell phones are getting any signal either. No cellular, no Wi-Fi. Not anywhere—up here, down there. Not even the visitor center at the entrance to the forest. We can't get through to our families. And it's not just communications, it's electricity too. Most of our stations up here work on generators. Those that don't are dark. No power. One of my staff said the credit card reader and pumps at the gas station up the highway even stopped working."

"Jesus," said the desk worker.

"Before we lost communications, we had several reports from our ranger stations. It started from our building at the southern entrance of the national forest. It's isolated there, but they have the best signal. They were picking up strange news stories. People were saying that there might have been some kind of attack on the grid in Washington. Cyber—I don't know exactly. Nobody does. At first, we thought it was just New England, but it turns out this may be all over the eastern seaboard."

"My God," said Doug.

The hiker lowered his voice and looked at him intently. "Last night I was hiking up along a ridgeline with a clear view west. The only town that way for thirty miles is Littleton. It's not a big place. Just a few trailer parks and a strip mall. But there was a huge fire. It looked like Walmart had gone up. I watched it for an hour, and it just burned. I don't think anybody came to put it out. One of our people said there was heavy traffic on I-91 and I-93. People driving north. The Canadian border is less than a hundred miles away."

"Why are people leaving the country?" said the desk worker.

"What steps are you taking?" asked Doug.

"Right now, we're just trying to account for everyone who's up in the mountains already. People hiking the Presidential Traverse, using the huts, registered in the system. Anybody who parked a car at a trailhead here in the national forest, we've got their license plate and name. There are day-hikers too. So we want to account for people. We want to keep people up high until they can go back down."

It took a moment for this to sink in. "Wait, keep people up in the mountains? People have planes to catch, families to get to, they want to tell loved ones they're safe—"

"Mister, they may not *be* safe."

Doug stopped and thought. He looked back at Tim, who looked up from his coloring and waved.

"How many of you are working on this? Ranger staff, I mean?"

"There're sixteen employees up here, as of today, and two supervisors, me and one other. We're trying to coordinate."

"And your name?"

"I'm Paul."

The desk worker asked, "Has anybody up at Mount Washington been able to get service? The visitor center has good

Wi-Fi, and the weather station has hard lines and Ethernet ports. They might be able to find out what's going on."

"I'm sure they've tried, but why don't you check in with Sarah or Mike up there and see what they've been able to find out. Use the CB. And Charlie—*don't sound panicked.* You don't know who may hear you." Paul turned to Doug as Charlie went into the office to make his call. "Look, I've got a million places to be, and I don't want to have to do this twice, so"—he gestured—"you want to take your boy outside for a minute, and I can talk to the group?"

TWO

An hour later their Danish friends arrived. They were smiling and laughing, tired from the day's march but glad in each other's company even after a twelve-mile hike. Linda, with her infectious grin, giggled with her daughter as they shared a bag of sweets. She and Ove both had fresh sun on their arms and foreheads and looked well for it. Not wishing to ruin their afternoon or still less their vacation, Doug had a thought to wait before delivering his news. He might allow them first to unpack and enjoy their meal—to linger for a few more moments in the glow of a sun-dappled day. But there was no avoiding the mood inside the cabin, which was charged with restless energy between the two staff members and the unsettled guests. And Linda and Ove might need to adjust their plans or make travel arrangements. They should be told at once. It would be false of him as their new friend not to do it.

It worked out that their boy and girl, Viggo and Sofia, both needed to use the toilet. Tim was in the camp's hammock, testing its strength and using it as a swing. As Ove walked up with a cheerful smile, Doug gathered him and his wife by placing a hand on each of their shoulders. Using a low voice, he spoke directly.

"My friends. I'm glad to see you. Good hike? Listen, I don't want to alarm you, but something's happened that you should know about. Down below the mountains. All the electrical and broadband in the area seems to have gone down. A ranger came through not long before you arrived. There may have been some kind of cyberattack. No one really knows what's going on."

The mirth slowly faded from Linda's face during this little speech, and Ove looked confused. "You are joking?" Linda asked.

Doug smiled tightly. "I'm afraid not."

"But what is it, exactly? Oh, this is going to interfere with the itinerary," she said with sudden frustration.

"I don't know," Doug said. "The supervising ranger's name is Paul. He's our age. A serious man. He seems to be in charge. We spoke. They are trying to account for all the hikers in the national forest. He said they can't get through to anyone who isn't on the mountain network. All the outside communications are down—no Wi-Fi, no cell service. Not even landlines. It's like a blackout all over northern New Hampshire. Or even beyond that." He repeated what Paul had told him and watched their faces fall.

"Do we tell the children?" Ove asked Linda.

"Tell them what?" she said. "It sounds like we don't know anything except that we're up here and the phones won't work down there." Ove got out his cell phone and began searching.

"No signal," he said.

"I don't plan to mention this to Tim for now," said Doug. "You guys do what you need to do. Your kids are a little older. But Tim would just have a million questions that I couldn't answer. I'm sure the power will come back on soon. For us, this might just mean that we extend our hiking trip a few days."

Ove smiled. "Nothing wrong with that."

"No planes," Linda said quietly.

"Sorry?"

"There haven't been any planes all day, did you notice? Yesterday we saw many and we looked at the vapor trails they made in the sky. Today not one."

Ove and Linda spoke to each other in Danish. Doug turned away and listened to their musical voices, marveling at the dense consonants and impenetrable clusters of sound. Like birds exchanging songs. Ove seemed unruffled but Linda sounded frustrated. After a conversation that lasted a few minutes, Linda said to Doug, "Let's see what else we can learn. We'd like to know a little more before we try to explain it to the children."

"This might turn out to be nothing," Doug said. "A fire at a Walmart and rumors getting out of control. And Wi-Fi crashes all the time. It's probably spotty up here to begin with. We just need to keep our heads." Ove nodded, eager at the idea. But Doug caught Linda's eye just before she turned and gazed at the sky again. She looked worried.

***

Tim was enjoying the hammock as Doug walked over. He lay across rather than in it, on his belly, and ran himself into a swinging motion as though he were on a playground. He wanted his father to watch as he went as high as he could and nearly tipped himself out onto his back at the top of his arc. Like some weightless jet describing a parabola. It was jarring, going from crisis and stress to childlike innocence like this. Tim had no notion that anything was wrong. Doug watched and tried to laugh along, using the child's self-absorption to his advantage. Even an empathetic boy had a limited universe with himself at the center.

"When's dinner?" he asked.

"About a half hour. Our friends are going to check in and pick their bunks."

"Are they going to sleep in our room?"

"Yep! I told them which one was ours and they're going to sleep there too."

"Good!" Tim shouted as he raced himself into motion once more.

"But I thought of something."

"What?"

"What if their dad snores?"

"Dad, *you* snore! And toot!"

"No, I don't! But *you* do!"

"Dad!"

***

At dinner, Doug positioned them so that Tim would sit next to Viggo, who was twelve. Doug hoped to facilitate some sort of interaction between the two boys, but they sat awkwardly, like assigned bus-mates on a school field trip. Conversation during the meal was stilted and brief. The adults did their best to maintain a veneer of good humor but found they had little small talk in them. The Danish children seemed to infer that something was wrong and exchanged a knowing glance. Unsettled by the mood at the table, Viggo and Sofia asked to be excused and went to the bunkroom to listen to their headphones. Tim sat a few minutes longer but then asked if he could play at one of the empty tables. Doug helped him retrieve his toy and get set up out of earshot. He returned to Linda and Ove.

"We were just discussing whether to cut things short and head home," Ove said.

"When were you originally planning to return?"

"Next Saturday. The children are on their autumn break from school this week. We were going to hike for two more days and fly to Chicago. Then back to New York and home via Paris. But maybe we skip Chicago and go back now. Try to drive north to Canada, rebook at the Montreal airport, and get home straight away."

"We don't want to be stranded on this side of the Atlantic," said Linda.

"Makes sense," said Doug. "It's probably nothing. But if this thing has affected airports, it could back up flights for weeks. It happened after 9/11—people got stuck. Probably easier to get a flight in Canada than New York right now."

"Yes," said Ove. But he seemed uncertain and rushed. He hesitated and then spoke again. "We also could wait and see a bit more before deciding."

"But we also don't want to waste time," said Linda impatiently. "Denmark isn't going to be involved in this, whatever it is. We are a small, quiet country. Nobody's hacking Denmark. I want to be with my parents, in my home. Not in the USA. People will be trying to get in and get out of here. Border crossings, airports, passport controls. It will be a nightmare. Waiting too long could mean we're stuck here or in Canada."

"Which wouldn't be too bad an alternative," said Ove. "I mean, Canada is safe, it's a friendly country—"

"And we don't *know* anybody there," Linda said in exasperation. She clearly wanted to leave as soon as possible.

"What are your plans?" asked Ove, turning to Doug. He seemed less comfortable than Linda in having a spousal disagreement in front of a relative stranger.

"Going to hold steady for the next few days. We were planning to keep hiking for the week anyway. With any luck, the power's back on by the time we finish. I don't want to overreact. But," he added quickly, "it's much simpler for us. We live just a few hundred miles away by car. It's more complicated when there are flights to catch and oceans to cross. And there's nothing waiting for us back home but an empty house, so we're in no rush to return."

He said more than he had intended. But his words softened Linda, who looked at him and then passed a careworn hand across her face.

"The boy sitting at the front desk said that Paul is going to hike down tomorrow and try to find out more. He's going to radio back up in the morning," said Ove.

"At least then we'll have some idea what's happening."

Outside it began to snow.

***

They waited until late morning before setting out for the Mount Washington observatory. It meant turning north once more and retracing their steps halfway back to Madison Spring. There still had been no news. An iron-gray sky had replaced the clear weather of the previous days. Half an inch of snow lay on the ground. Doug had slept poorly and rose well before dawn, sitting in the darkness of the great room with his coffee. Part of him wanted to continue with his own itinerary, carrying on while the problem resolved itself. But a greater part did not want to be left behind. The boy had been right: it was hard to make friends, and here was friendship. In the face of uncertainty, it was better to band together than remain alone. As they had been for so many years. The young woman who had helped Tim select a brownie the day before emerged in the kitchen before the sun rose. Her name was Kate. She said she had slept beside the radio. She had received no updates other than worried-sounding reports from the other high huts counting guests' heads. Paul had begun his hike down to the base at four thirty that morning by the light of his headlamp. "We'll know more soon," Kate said. "He moves fast. How's Tim?" she asked, remembering the boy's name.

The waiting and uncertainty affected the three adults in Doug's party differently. Linda packed and prepared, eager to take the next step. She cinched stuff sacks and backpack straps with a briskness that betrayed her impatience. The children's bowls were off the table and cleaned practically as they ate their last spoonfuls. She needed to be in motion even if she did not know what step to take. Her good humor had been replaced by pragmatism. Ove took a more philosophical approach and seemed able to put the situation out of mind. Outwardly, his mood and outlook appeared fundamentally the same. He seemed determined to enjoy the cold alpine morning. Doug thought he did so for the sake of the children. From breakfast onward he occupied himself with Viggo and Sofia, taking them on a short morning hike toward nearby Mount Pierce. He presented the weather as a lucky opportunity and said they would use the overnight snow to look for fresh animal tracks. Tim declined an offer to join them, citing the chilly morning air. For his part, Doug struggled to balance contingency planning with the futility of worry. He tried to think ahead but found there were so many possibilities that he ended up fretting uselessly. There was no point in planning ten steps in the future when events would dictate the next five. The situation was fundamentally out of his control, and he knew that in all likelihood it would resolve before their trek ended. Yet committing to a posture of equanimity required constant discipline. He frequently caught himself wandering into the territory of handwringing, as he had fallen into the habit of doing while parenting alone. He offered to play chess with Tim, having discovered a board on a bookshelf crowded with old paperbacks and games. They played. Tim was too young to make a competitive match, but Doug could create a challenge in setting traps that his son could exploit to win and build confidence.

When no report arrived by ten o'clock, Linda pressed Ove for their family to set out. Mount Washington was the highest point not just in the White Mountain National Forest but in the northeastern United States. It was in the center of the wilderness but also more accessible to outsiders than other huts in the Presidential Traverse. The peak was high enough to be foreboding but not so high as to be out of reach even to a party with children. Mount Washington's weather was famously treacherous, and for a century its summit had held the world's highest wind speed record on land. There was a weather observatory there, and it was possible to reach the summit by car or cog railway during the tourist season that had recently ended. The summit had no overnight hut for backpackers. Yet the infrastructure that supported scientists and tourists included a large building, a cafeteria, a gift shop, electricity, and flush toilets, as well as cellular and Wi-Fi service. Linda argued that rather than waiting in backcountry isolation, they should go to the central point in the traverse with the best communications and quickest access down to the base. Many others would doubtless be there, and they would find the most opportunities for gathering news and information. Doug thought, but did not say, that he would prefer to stay away from others and the panicked energy they might bring to the children. But at the time their need for information seemed as pressing as any other concern. And Doug wanted to stay close to the Danish family so that he could have decision-making partners in the coming hours.

***

Reaching the summit of Mount Washington was possible but would be a serious undertaking. Doug and Tim had avoided it earlier in their journey, both to keep away from crowds of tourists and because the route was so arduous. It was a hike rather than any sort of technical climb. Danger lay not in falling into oblivion but in exposure to the elements and exhaustion for the boy. The overnight snow would make an ascent more difficult still. It was only seven miles from their cabin to the summit, but with a trail elevation gain of almost four thousand feet and unbroken exposure to wind. This would make it their most challenging day to date. They did not have the benefit of a weather forecast. It was a risk. The adults discussed whether to wait and set out the following morning. But Linda would not stay any longer.

As they began their hike, Tim asked why they were turning back in the direction from which they had come. "We have a chance to see from the top of Mount Washington," Doug said. "So we're going to join our new friends and go there. We will be able to see for a hundred miles!" Like much that he had told his son over the past twelve hours, this was perfectly true but also incomplete. He did not want to lie to the boy if he could help it.

"How long are we hiking today?"

"It's only seven miles, but it will be mostly uphill."

"Seven miles is about half of what we did yesterday, right? Because that was twelve miles?"

"That's right. But remember how some of that was downhill."

"Will we sleep at Mount Washington?"

"Yes. It's bigger at the top of that mountain than at the other cabins."

"Will there be brownies like yesterday?"

"I think they have even more food than this cabin. They might even have chips."

The weather was colder. The two family groups each fell into step slightly apart from one another, with Doug and Tim in the back. Linda set an aggressive pace that seemed impossible to sustain. For a time the others tried to match it, but she began to pull away. More than once Tim asked why they were walking so fast. Doug said they had gotten a late start and wanted to make it to the summit before dark. When they asked Linda to stop for water after an hour, Doug spoke with her quietly.

"We're not going to be able to keep up with you at this rate."

"We've got to hurry. We didn't set out until almost noon."

"Tim is only seven, Linda. His legs are short, and he gets tired quickly."

"I'll try to slow down. But we had better get ourselves there before dark."

"Do you think we might not?"

"Depends on how many breaks we take. Almost ready?" She said this last to the group at large, in a louder, peremptory voice. They had only just stopped. Tim seemed badly winded. Doug looked at her angrily, but she was already moving again. When Ove began to pass, looking tired but resolute, Doug took him aside for a private word. "Tim and I may need to turn back. We're not going to be able to keep going at Linda's speed."

Ove studied his face for a moment. "I'll get in front and lead for a while. That slows us down. She always goes fast. We stick together, hey?" He smiled and placed a reassuring hand on Doug's shoulder.

They marched onward throughout the afternoon with Ove in front. The wind picked up in the high shoulder between Mounts Eisenhower and Monroe. They were past the halfway point. The way out now was through. Doug tried to fortify the boy with extra rations of chocolate, which Tim ate in silence. Had it been just the two of them, he would likely have complained. He did not want to be the weak link in the group. Doug's right knee began to ache and a hot spot was forming above his heel. Ordinarily he would have stopped to treat and bandage it before a blister formed. But there was no time. Reaching the summit became the only goal. Thinking beyond to the comfort of his feet for subsequent days' hiking was a distant worry. They passed another mountain hut but saw no one and did not stop. Their boots carried them forward. They made their way like soldiers in a platoon. As their feet and limbs grew tired and then numb, every step moved them further through the high mountain air. Each was lost in thought. They retreated from conversing, or admiring the view, or looking for wildlife and allowed their bodies to continue performing the motions that were necessary. Walking was their first and only business. In its service, they breathed and watched the ground for rocks or other obstacles. Their heads kept down like animals. It was hard, pure, monotonous, unequivocal work. Then the mountain appeared.

The large hulking presence of the massif came into view as they cut around Mount Monroe. Loose rock and scree carved out paths and gullies along its flanks. Mount Washington was huge and symmetrical, obstructing light as an iceberg displaces the sea. Its flat summit formed a broad plateau. They had seen it at other points in their journey, but never face to face. The top quarter of the mountain stood there, impassive to the travelers' presence and indifferent to their small human crisis. Thankfully, their traverse had inched them up to a high elevation, leaving only 2,500 feet of Washington left to climb. They could manage it in a few hours. It was hardly the Himalayas or even the Rockies. But it was all upward, exposed and without reprieve. It would be difficult on the boy. Doug gazed up in fear and wonder. In the mountain's shadow, the air blew cold and fast.

When Linda tightened the hip belt on her pack and set out to begin her climb, Doug made a decision. He knew it was what his wife Carol would have done. The summit was in view and well within reach. "You go ahead," he said. "Tim and I are going to have a break here, catch our breath, have some food, and take our time going up."

Ove made to stay but a sharp glance from Linda caused him to hesitate. Doug shook his head in earnest appeal. "Really. It's just for the final stretch. There's no danger. You could watch us come up behind you the entire way. You've got more legs left than we have. We can do it, but we need to go slower. We'll meet you."

Ove walked over, looking concerned. "You are sure about this? I think we should stick together."

"We're slowing you down. It's pretty clear Linda wants to get there right away. And besides, there might be some benefit to arriving in stages."

Ove studied him and understood. "OK. It might be best if I come find you at the top. This way you don't need to bring Tim into any situation you wish him to avoid. In case it's crowded there, or—whatever."

"I don't know the layout at the summit. I'm not sure where we would meet."

"Neither do I." He gazed above them. Thin whisps of cloud blew by quickly. A weather tower extended several stories above the other structures that they could see from their vantage point. "See that white tower? I'll get us set up someplace where we can see the bottom of that. I will keep an eye out for you and come out to you when you arrive."

"My friend," Doug said, taking him by the shoulder and giving it a little shake.

Ove looked at him closely, assessing his strength. Doug could see the stubble on his chin and cheeks, blondish white like a surfer's on a long weekend. "You are feeling well enough? It's safe to leave you, you can both make it to the top?"

"Yes. We've got it in us. We just can't go as fast and will do better if we can rest a bit first."

"Tim is OK?" The boy was sitting and slowly eating an energy bar.

"He's seen tougher days than this."

"OK, then we will meet soon. Bonne chance," said Ove. "I'll be looking back to check on your progress. Keep your bright red shell on so I can spot you. Use your whistle if you run into trouble. Three pulses, like so, *ta-ta-taaaaa*, means I come back. Or you wave your arms crosswise like this, and I come to you. Yes?" He set out after his family, who had already advanced fifty yards up the winding trail.

✳✳✳

"Dad?" Tim asked.

"Yeah, buddy?"

"I'm tired."

"I know. It's been a long day, hasn't it?"

"Is everything alright?"

"What do you mean?"

"It seems like Viggo's mom and dad are nervous. You keep talking to them and I can't hear what you're saying. And they walk too fast."

Doug looked at the boy and said, "There seems to be something wrong with everybody's phones. Nothing is really working. So we're all trying to figure out what's going on."

"Oh. Maybe they should turn them off and back on again. That sometimes works."

"Good idea."

"Is that all that's wrong?"

Doug hesitated. "There was a fire down below. The people who worked at the last hut saw it while they were hiking."

"Where was the fire?"

"It was at a store near the mountains."

"Could it burn down the mountain?"

"No."

"But what about the trees? Couldn't they catch fire?"

"Trees can catch fire, that's true. But not the whole mountain."

"OK."

"One of the reasons we came to Mount Washington is to find out more. We want to make sure it's safe before we go back down. So we're sticking with our new friends, and we're going up to this observatory, where we can see a lot better, and where we can hopefully get some more information."

"Do they have Wi-Fi here?"

"I'm not sure."

"And you said there'd be chips."

"I *hope* so."

"I hope they have Cool Ranch."

"*I* hope they have Fritos."

"But can we rest before we start hiking again?"

"You bet, pal. What time have you got?"

Tim looked at his watch. He held it close to his nose and studied the hands intently before saying that it was 3:37.

"Why don't we hang out here until four? Want to hear a story?"

"Yeah."

Doug lay down on his back in the hollow of several boulders. His son nestled into the crook of his arm, resting his head on his father's chest. In this space, there was a reprieve from the wind. Doug draped his puffy coat facedown over them both, each of them placing an arm in a sleeve. As they lay there, he spun a tale about Chuck the Silly Brown Dog. He was the hero of the boy's favorite series of books who lived a life of luxury and constantly found new ways to get into mischief. When they didn't have a book from the series at hand, he would make up a story. Together they would come up with various doings of ancillary characters like Chuck's beloved brother James, his slow silly owners, and the dog Jojo who lived next door and whom Chuck understood to be his best friend. Even exhausted, Tim could not hold still for more than a few moments and squirmed as Doug improvised a story about Chuck winning a skiing contest.

They lost themselves in the narrative. He watched the boy's reactions. Where he made jokes and hoped for laughter, he received only a wan smile. Tim's smaller body breathed at a faster pace than his father's. Freckles across the boy's nose and cheeks had come out from several days' exposure to the sun. He always sunburned first directly beneath his lower eyelids. Sandy hair lay across his forehead and covered the tops of his ears. As Tim yawned, Doug saw his adult incisors coming in, disproportionately large in his childlike jaw. Somehow the scent of his breath retained an undercurrent of innocence no matter what he had eaten. A fragrance of milk teeth and dreaming. His hands were beginning to hint at the shape they would carry into manhood. The index fingers bent inward toward their fellows at the same middle knuckle as his own. He slipped a hand into Tim's and the boy held it loosely. When the story ended, they watched clouds pass by quickly above, pencil-gray in the overcast weather. That one looks like an elephant, said Tim. That one looks like a banana, said Doug. That one looks like Mom, Tim said.

***

He encouraged the boy to lead the push to the summit. The going was not as hard as he had remembered, with little hand-over-foot scrambling. But the steady incline never slackened. There were no flats or any depressions in the path. If they needed a reprieve, they must stop walking. When he had last hiked these trails, he had been a young man. Even then, the going had been hard. They both overheated quickly and began to shed layers. He stuffed gloves and hats into pockets and clipped gaiters to the outside of backpacks so that they would not have to remove and reshoulder their heavy burdens. At a certain point, all became momentum and the drive to complete their ascent. He told his son he was strong. This was both a statement and an act. Hearing this assurance from his father lent him strength and gave added force to his movements. They climbed.

He kept an eye on the approaching peak, but it disappeared from time to time and eventually was lost to sight. He could not see anyone looking down on their progress. After ninety minutes a false summit caused them to stop in exasperation and take a break for water and food. The boy's determination was mixed with pride, and he wanted to press on and finish the day's hike. It was growing dark. Doug was likewise ready to continue but did not want the boy to exhaust himself. He pled fatigue and asked if he could have a few more moments to gather his reserves for the final push. They drank water. He watched his credulous son's pity for him as he pantomimed windedness. In a few years' time, he would no longer have to manufacture this dynamic. Nor would he care to. Tim's expression was mostly empathy and patience, but Doug perceived also a grace note of exultation as he reveled in what he perceived to be his own superior strength. Like one runner passing another. Like a farmhand who has broken a horse. After two minutes more they resumed their path over the boulder field.

A shocking blast of Arctic wind greeted them at the summit. Doug raised an arm to shield his eyes from the vortex, and Tim reeled and looked as though he might just blow away. The violent sound of the wind in their ears and the rippling fabric of their jackets drowned out every other sensation. They linked arms and leaned forward into the gale. After a few yards, they sheltered in the lee of a huge cairn of rocks marking the very zenith of the mountain and capped with a sign displaying its name and altitude. This cut the wind and allowed Doug to orient himself to the summit's layout. In spite of themselves, they laughed and whooped in exultation. Doug told his son that he was proud of him.

The summit was a broad plateau the size of a grammar school campus. A large building dominated the space. It doubled as observatory and tourist center, as well as a weather station. In the dusk its yellow lights served as a beacon. The observatory featured long curved walls set at obtuse angles and rounded corners, with one parapet or lookout tower standing taller than the rest in the fashion of a lighthouse. A sturdy white weather tower stood apart from this building and rose above it, anchored by steel guylines. They could see the tracks for the cog railway that would bring tourists up and down the mountainside in the summer. A road wound up and around the far slope of the mountain to an empty parking lot. They were just past the peak of foliage season and well into fall, when the summit remained open to drivers but was used mainly by meteorological staff. Ove was standing at the base of the weather tower, layered in cold-weather gear and shuffling to keep warm. They walked to him, once more out in the wind. As they approached, he gave a broad smile to them and made a show of congratulating Tim on his ascent of the mountain, praising his efforts and endurance. He had to shout to be heard over the wind. They sheltered next to the weather tower.

"Any news?" Doug asked.

Ove shook his head almost imperceptibly and gestured toward Tim. *Not in front of the boy.* "We are all set up inside, where it's warm. I'll show you. They have a cafeteria with hot chocolate, Tim, and warm soup."

"Do they have chips?"

Ove laughed. "I think so. Just about everything—we ate until we almost burst! They have candy bars also. You like chocolate?"

"Yep," Tim said. His voice was tiny next to the roar of the mountain.

They made their way inside. The door closed behind them and sealed off the outer world of wind and violence. Inside was an entirely different space than the alpine huts of the past few nights. Here at the top of New England they had somehow returned to civilization. There were linoleum floors and electric lights, restrooms with flush toilets, and doors and walls made of glass and steel rather than the rough and ready materials of the wild. The cabins and their make-do outhouses and picnic tables were a thing apart. Signage overhead directed visitors down various hallways to the cafeteria, information center, observation deck, and cog railway platform. A familiar yellow plastic sign warned that an area of the floor was slippery when wet. The chug of a generator came from below. It was disorienting after nearly a week in the backcountry, like stepping into a bright afternoon after time spent in a dark theater. They both found the space off-putting.

"The cafeteria is down that way, and that's where some other people are," Ove said, looking at Doug meaningfully. "It was rather noisy in there, so we found ourselves a nice space that's a little bit away from the din. They don't have sleeping quarters here, so we just found an unused room that's got carpeting on the floors and set up there. More comfortable for the sleeping bags than lying on the lino floor," he smiled. "It's this way, just follow me down the hall. Great view out these windows, Tim."

The room looked like a college classroom or modest conference space. Business tables and chairs had been moved against a wall to make room for the family's things. Linda, Viggo, and Sofia were there, sitting on the floor playing cards. They had stacked their backpacks neatly and already set up their sleeping bags. Remnants of a meal lay in a wastepaper bin near the door. Linda smiled in a relieved way as they entered, stood, and wordlessly walked over to embrace Tim and Doug in turn. She was very tender with the boy, smoothing his hair and whispering gentle conspiracies. He plainly enjoyed the mothering. He did not fight against her caresses as he would do if Doug tried to show the same affection. As Linda hugged Doug, she kissed his cheek and whispered in his ear, "I'm sorry." She looked at him directly and he nodded. Her eyes were shining, and he reassured her.

"Listen. We both needed to do what was best for our families. I'm glad we're all together again."

Ove showed Tim where to set up his things and handed
him a cold sports drink. The boy sat down and drank in gulps.
Then Ove made a show of asking what they would like from
the cafeteria. Tim requested chips and a chocolate bar, as well
as pizza if they had any. Doug joined Linda and Ove while their
children moved over and sat near Tim to talk about their ascent.
His mountaineering seemed to have won him new respect with
the teenagers. They were uncommonly solicitous whereas before
they had shown little interest. Perhaps their good parents had
instructed them to make friends. Sofia showed off a dark red
blister on the side of her big toe. The three set about compar-
ing scars like old sailors passing a bottle.

"Buddy, I'm just going to find out what kind of food they
have at the cafeteria," Doug said. "We'll be right here in the
hallway talking for a few minutes." Tim barely noticed. The
three adults stepped around the corner. The faces of the Danes
were grave.

"Still no phones," said Linda. "They don't have Wi-Fi or
cellular here either. They've got electricity from backup generators, so at least we won't be cold. And the cafeteria is working.
It sounds like this man Paul that you met has not yet returned.
A woman called Jane is in charge. She is in the cafeteria."

"There are many other people there as well," said Ove.
"Hikers. People from all over the traverse have gathered. I was
talking to a few. Some of them had screenshots on their phones
from before power went out. Not good, Doug."

"Tell me."

"It's not just some conspiracy website. They had real news

stories. There has been a huge cyberattack on the USA. It hit all over, at once, two days ago. Government agencies, defense, bureaucracy, but also industry and telecommunications. Energy pipelines. Electrical grids. All the major providers of broadband and fiber-optics service were affected. Some of the news articles ended midsentence."

"What, like all at once? Who did it?"

"One thing I saw said it was too sophisticated for terrorism or hackers. It had to be another government. Russia, China, Iran—something like that."

"Another article talked about some cyberattack by Russia against Ukraine years ago," said Linda. "They disabled the country's entire electricity supply. But this is much bigger."

"Is it only the US?"

"Yes, they say so," said Ove. "But it's all over the country, not just here in the east."

"Are you telling me you can't make a phone call anywhere in America right now?" Doug was astonished.

Linda spoke up again and made him realize how little he understood the situation. "It's much worse than that. You can't turn on a light switch anywhere in the USA right now. The whole country is dark."

***

The soup burned his tongue and throat on the way down. He hardly noticed. Mushrooms and wild rice in broth. There was coffee as well. It warmed him from the inside as he ate and drank, but he tasted little. Tim had a stronger appetite for his pizza. For once he was not picky about how much sauce was under the cheese. He had two slices of pepperoni, pausing only to stuff in more chips, and washed it all down with his sports drink. The cafeteria was well stocked. Its staff were on site and working, so they continued making food for the thirty or so people holed up at the summit observatory. Doug and Tim ate sitting beside each other, leaning against the wall next to their things. They had unrolled their sleeping bags and pillows and set out their toiletries. Carol had always said that spending the night in a strange place feels better once the bed is made. Tim's spaceship toy stood ready to play, although he was sensitive to how Sofia and Viggo would view it. "Kids want older kids to think they're cool, Dad," he told his father.

Darkness covered the mountain. The wind had picked up and howled past in fierce bursts. It carried spindrift with it and denuded the summit plateau of most snow. Their room had no windows and they heard only the loudest gusts. The observatory was well fortified. They sat in their alpine shelter like sequestered jurors. There had been more news in the hallway, but for now it was a confused blur. Gray photos of iconic skylines, suddenly deprived of light. Runs on supermarkets and gun stores. Lines for gas with siphons used to fill plastic buckets. Gatherings of revelers, or protesters, or mobs, in Central Park and Boston Common. Backed up highways. Lines of police behind clear plastic riot shields. Fires burning out of control. The president and vice president kept apart to ensure the continuity of government. It all seemed so distant and hypothetical here on top of the mountain, under fluorescent cylinder bulbs of all things. The one place where power still flowed.

Tim could sense something wrong but did not know what it was. His confused tone reflected a lack of understanding of events that were at any rate being kept from him. He looked into his father's face for clues but saw only unaccountable stress and worry. Trying to compensate or to move events into happier territory, he adopted a tone of saccharine whimsy that tended to grate. Linda and Ove had been wise to find space for the two families away from the cafeteria, where harried conversations and the occasional argument filled the air. For the sake of all three children, it was better to form a bubble and control the flow of information. Yet they decided that, as often as possible, one adult from their party should remain in the common area to monitor developments. If someone arrived at the observatory with critical news, or a group left to try their fortunes elsewhere, or word of a storm came, they must know. They rotated this task and Doug took a turn as Sofia began teaching Tim a card game. She was performing a kindness but also seemed to mildly enjoy the open-faced adulation she received from the boy. Linda was resting with her head on Ove's leg, and they talked quietly in Danish like mourners back from a funeral. Viggo wore his headphones. Doug did not know to what extent Linda and Ove had shared the bizarre news with their two children.

As he walked down the long hallway between their room and the cafeteria, he had a few moments' solitude. He had not had much time to himself since he and Tim had begun the trip. The boy did not bring the same expectations for constant conversation that an adult companion might have. Still, the two of them chatted on and off all day. Tim's need to satisfy any urge or thought the moment it arose meant frequent changes of subject or tone, often with a pressing note. Maintaining a veneer of fatherly interest and patience took an effort, especially when the topic was a new idea for what the boy would request for his birthday, or a new description of a comic book villain or hero. Tim was moody and could suddenly plummet, exhausting his parent. But he also had greater stores of resilience than his father and bounced back from a low moment more quickly, often outpacing Doug, for whom the storm lingered. And the boy had a bottomless store of charm. The effort of managing it all added up, and Doug could have used a true reprieve. He had not anticipated the effect of so much compressed time together when planning the trip. It had been an attempt to put away screens and instill the same love of the outdoors that had meant so much to him. To escape the downsized house that still did not feel like home. At least for a few days. In his ordinary working life, Doug's occupation was independent. He could spend hours at a time working at his desk, dealing with colleagues over e-mail, and avoiding phone calls in a solitary or near-solitary state. With Tim off at school, he would find himself passing entire days speaking to no one at all. Recently when he had said hello to a fellow parent picking up his child at the ring of the school bell, his voice came out in a hoarse croak. The last time he had spoken was eight hours earlier when he had wished the boy a good day.

And now he had a quiet moment to contemplate what felt like an unraveling. There was no telling the scope of this disruption or its ramifications. It was important not to overreact. Yet without a sounding board, he found himself reaching for historical reference points, well beyond the American catastrophe on 9/11 and to the great crises of earlier generations: the first and second World Wars, the Great Depression, the Spanish influenza, even the Civil War. Allowing his mind to wander in this way felt melodramatic and overblown. But he had no way to grasp the reach of what was underway. None of them did. Was this a hiccup in the power supply that would be over in a few days' time? Or at the other extreme, the cyberattack might prefigure some sort of military conflict. First take out the power, then bring war. He had no idea whether the country's defenses were prepared for something like this. Did the military have backup generators for their radars? Their anti-aircraft batteries? Their submarines? As he walked and let his thoughts unfold, he felt himself grow tense with worry. He no longer had a partner to check his impulses or talk him down. His thoughts spun freely, like a car without brakes careening down a hill. He was doing it again: surrendering to anxiety and letting it take him where it would. This was the difference between having a partner and being alone. It was like the time when he decided to alphabetize the CD collection. All the music was now digital; the CDs were in boxes gathering dust. But no one was there to tell him to stop. To the contrary, Tim had taken an interest in the tactility of the shining discs and their cases and had sat down to help. The project accomplished nothing. He returned to the problem at hand. Maybe the external damage had been done and the next step would be for the country to shred itself. It was already bitterly divided; here was the chance for cultural and political disagreement to break out into open conflict at last. With no one to restore order—to answer a police radio call or organize the national guard—conditions in the cities could deteriorate quickly. Cities like Boston.

Something Paul had said to him the previous day had stayed at the top of mind. It may not be safe to descend. Their home was in a large city that relied on networks and infrastructure to maintain safe working order. Returning to it without power or protection of any kind might be foolish. All they had to keep the world at bay were the locks on their doors. He had no gun for self-defense. There was no electricity for the home security system. No one would answer the call even if the alarm was tripped. The windows were single panes of glass, shattered as easily as the clapping of hands. And where would they get their food? Potable water? Without basic urban systems that he had always taken for granted, none of these things would exist. The plumbing would stop working. His white-collar job would become unnecessary. Their position seemed precarious. They had no possessions other than what they carried and what sat in their car parked at the trailhead—if it had not been ransacked or stolen. They had become high-altitude refugees. A portable family. They could start over somewhere, he thought wildly. Perhaps this was the moment to leave the only country he had ever inhabited. It was a step he had considered more than once since Carol had died, but never with any seriousness of purpose. He wondered what Linda and Ove would do. If they could cross the Atlantic, they would find their way back to Denmark. Maybe Doug and Tim should join them. It was a small, presumably nonaligned country, wealthy, safe, sensibly run, of little strategic interest. Yet the Nazis had occupied Denmark during World War II, hadn't they—much as they occupied other parts of conquered Europe? There was nothing to say that the continent would not become a pawn in this conflict too, menaced by larger powers and even less safe than the US for being small and relatively defenseless.

They could flee to Canada. Its grid did not seem to have been attacked. Canada was nearby and vast. A great ocean separated it from any potential adversaries. They could withdraw into Alberta or British Columbia and find a small mountain town, as he had always wanted to do in America. A family could start over there. But an asterisk followed Doug through this way of thinking. It meant getting across the border. One of the articles that Ove had read on his phone mentioned the closure of the Canadian and Mexican borders to noncitizens, and particularly to American migrants. Globalization was reversing. Walls and nations reappeared, as though they had never really vanished. A US passport—once the most sought-after credential on the international market—had lost its value. So getting into Canada would mean crossing illegally. It was a risk, especially with a young child in tow. They would have to find their way through the mountains at some unguarded section of the frontier and walk across. And then they would live stateless and in fear, without visas or immigration papers. They could be arrested and deported back into a lawless country. Canada would never separate a child from his parent—or would it? If it faced an influx of migrants during a war it might have to adjust its policy and leave behind its wholesome image to create deterrence. He would not take the risk.

He felt his intrinsic caution and conservatism taking over. His instinct was usually to resist change, to put off action: to weigh and re-weigh risks until the moment of opportunity had passed. He would never have succeeded in business. Seeing around corners and spotting trends was not his talent. This had always frustrated Carol. He was unable to act until he had marinated each option while she stood ready to take the first step and deal with consequences in turn. Yet in a crisis, perhaps caution and prudence were better. What use was leaping out into the blue when the remade world could be treacherous? They knew so little about events, just what scraps they had been able to glean from phones and snatched conversations with others. He had friends in western Massachusetts, in the Berkshires. They would be welcome there. But how to travel safely? They could drive—but only if there was enough fuel in the tank to cross half of New England. They could not rely on gas stations along the way. They might be empty or unusable. Doug tried to recall when he had most recently put fuel in the car and failed to remember. And if their car was gone, making such a journey on foot would take weeks. Where would they sleep? What would they eat? What dangers would they face on the road? The civil unrest Linda and Ove had mentioned might prevent an overland journey of so many miles.

Perhaps the safest option, Doug thought, was staying in the one place where the uncertainty seemed unlikely to reach them: here in the mountains. At least for the next few days. It felt absurd to make such life-altering decisions against an abstract threat. But whether or not he could see it, the danger was there. He reflected. They were in a location of no great interest to anyone. The nearest major American city was Boston, two hundred miles to the south. Equidistant to the northwest was Montreal: a hub of vibrant culture but not a capital or a center of industry, even supposing Canada were to be drawn into any sort of conflict. If a traditional war did follow, there seemed no reason for anyone to set up a position in the White Mountains. It was in the middle of nowhere, far north of the major cities of the eastern seaboard, and well west of the Atlantic. In an era of laser-guided missiles and precision bombs, the commanding heights were no longer needed to spot targets. At any rate, both Boston and Montreal seemed far enough away to make the Presidential Range strategically useless. It was not like the Alps straddling a border between Italy and Austria in the 1940s. Of all the locations on their journey, the Mount Washington summit and observatory was the most prominent and accessible point because of its infrastructure and the access road. It was therefore the most likely to appeal to some hypothetical faction or army. But even that was a stretch. A soldier standing on a mountaintop glassing the valley with binoculars was far less effective than drones and satellites.

He stopped himself. These thoughts were ridiculous. He was planning for World War III when all he really knew was that the lights had been switched off. They might already be back on again. These contingencies were fifty steps ahead of what he needed to decide: whether to continue the hike or cut it short. Whether to stop along the way or drive straight home. How to help his new friends reach *their* home. Still. A thought tickled his mind and he could not repress it. He allowed himself to play out the question of whether they could survive a winter above the tree line. If they had to. If the lights stayed off and order broke down. The weather would be ferocious. Meters of snow. Dreadful storms and wind. They would be cut off from the world below. Hiking in or out from, say, mid-November through mid-March would be a measure of last resort, especially with the boy. Even if they reached the bottom, they would be stranded in a huge wilderness, miles from any town. The backcountry huts did not have electric or gas heating, so they would need to use one of the huts with a fireplace and stock it with fuel for their warmth. How would they provision? Were there enough food stores to sustain a man and a boy for six months? A year? If not, could he hunt? He didn't have a rifle and had hardly fired a gun in his life. He had never dressed game before. Would they be alone or would others stay as well? Would the wardens even allow them to stay—to become squatters, unable to pay beyond the currency of their own labor? He had no idea if they typically closed up the backcountry huts for the winter. Maybe they allowed skiers to use them. Having live-in wardens to do any upkeep, radio control, or trail maintenance surely had some benefit. He rolled the thoughts over in his head as he walked slowly. His reflection followed him along the hallway windows' darkening glass.

***

Approaching the cafeteria, he heard the din of conversation but no arguments or raised voices. The day was winding down. Families and hiking groups had arranged spots for themselves in the large open space. Some had even pitched their tents, providing a modicum of privacy and recreating the cocoon feel of a campsite. Several meals were coming to an end, and the kitchen staff were cleaning and closing up their stations. A large fire burned in the central hearth, the one feature common to both the observatory and the backcountry huts. Yet, in this in-dustrial space, the fire was ornamental rather than a source of vital warmth. Coffee was on, and Doug walked over and poured himself a mug. He wrapped his fingers around it, warming them on the hot ceramic as he surveyed the area. People looked tired and anxious. There was a note of uncertainty about the eyes of the trekkers, hard to describe but distinct. Mistrust hung in the room like an odor. Who can I count on? each pair of eyes seemed to ask. Such misgivings were uncommon among hikers.

It was a self-selecting group of people, usually friendly, of a like mind politically, and eager to chip in and help out. Granted, there were occasional alpha males who looked down on those with the wrong gear or a slower pace. But the tone among those encountered on a trail or in a backcountry lodge was open and warm. Now the common element in the room was suspicion. Whenever he made eye contact with anyone, even momentarily, as he looked from table to table, they looked away quickly. The instinct to connect, so integral to the mountain lifestyle, had suddenly disappeared. It was apparently that precarious. Everyone seemed to want to keep to themselves, stay away from unnecessary risks, and avoid taking chances.

He noticed a woman seated at one of the cafeteria tables giving directions to two observatory staff members. She spoke with quiet authority and gestured with a carpenter's pencil. Doug thought she must be the other supervising ranger that Linda had mentioned. She seemed to be in her late thirties: lean, fit, with a pretty face and hands that had spent time on rock. Her sunworn skin was lighter around the eyes, suggesting months of eye protection at altitude, and her manicured eyebrows were her one concession to vanity. A handheld radio sat on the table before her. As he watched, the staff members left, and she began making a count of the guests and recording it in a notepad. A half-eaten bowl of chili sat on the table. Unlike the hikers in their indoor shoes, she was still wearing boots and an outdoor jacket, unzipped. Doug walked over and sat down across from her.

"What's the latest?" he asked.

She looked up. "Didn't you hear the announcement?"

"My group is down the hall. My son and I. We've got young

children; we're staying in another room, so they don't pick up on too much of what is going on. Don't want them getting too frightened. I'm Doug," he said, reaching a hand across the table and maintaining eye contact. He did not want to be turned away without learning anything.

She didn't shake hands but gave a tired half smile. "Jane. I think I met another member of your party earlier. Well, Doug," she said with a sigh, "the latest is that we've got a big group that's going to be hiking out in the morning, and I'm trying to get everything organized."

"How many?"

"Most. We've got thirty-nine people at the observatory, not counting me. So far, twenty-six are planning to head out."

"And go where?"

"Home."

"Do you really think that's a smart idea?"

"Not up to me. It's a free country. I can't keep someone up here if they want to leave. People want to get back to their homes, their families. It's my job to help them get down safely."

"Which way will you be hiking out?"

"We're going to go straight down Washington. Tuckerman Ravine Trail. Once we descend, there's a shuttle system—or there used to be—at the base that runs between trailheads throughout the national forest. Route 16. Hike people out and then use the bus to get them to their cars at the various trailhead parking lots. Send them on their way."

"So a one-day hike out, is that the idea?"

"Yes. It's a long day, hiking down Washington, but it's doable. We've got a wide range of fitness levels. Some of them will be on that bus for a while afterward, but at least everybody will be at their car before dark. Unfortunately, the cog railway is shut down. Otherwise, we'd just ride down."

"Couldn't you start it up again—the railway?"

"The railway car is stored at the base of the mountain, not the peak. And anyway, I don't think it works anymore, after the surge."

"So that's what they're calling it."

"I don't think anybody knows what to call it."

"Strange times."

"That's for sure."

"Do you know if the cars at the trailheads are still there?"

"Why wouldn't they be?"

"I don't know, looters. Smash a car window, hot-wire an engine."

"This far north? Hardly anybody lives around here."

"Walmart was on fire. If I'm raiding a Walmart, I might start thinking about all the Subarus and 4Runners parked at the White Mountain trailheads. Lot of wealth parked in this forest. And not much else to steal around here."

"Maybe. I'll have a ranger cruise by the nearest lot before we set out and see if anything looks out of place. We don't want to end up down there with thirty people on a bus and nowhere to put them."

"Assuming the cars are there," Doug said, "people just get in and . . . start driving?"

"You seem to think I can decide whether people stay or go. But our responsibility ends at the edge of the national forest."

"Right, but you're sending them *out* of the national forest, tired, at dusk, with no idea what's out there. Someone gets a flat tire, someone hits a roadblock, who knows. People could get hurt."

"Look, man, it's not up to me," Jane said impatiently as she put down her pencil. "We're not Triple A. Most of the people up here are desperate to get back to their homes, their families. You said your son is with you? That couple over there has two kids in Philadelphia home with a sitter. They need to get back to them. While you were in your private room, I just spent an hour persuading a group not to hike out *tonight*. Somebody wants to pull a stunt like that on the mountain, we've got some sway and can intervene. But we have no right to keep anybody in the national forest. It's not our call. If they want to leave, we can help them get down the mountain safely. And if you take my advice, you and your son should go tomorrow too."

"Hike out with the others."

"If you don't, you're on your own. I may not come back up afterward—me or my staff. I don't know anything beyond the next eighteen hours."

"How long can you stay up here?"

"What, like through the weekend?"

"Maybe longer."

She gave him a sharp look. "Not long. This place gets fierce when the weather turns, and it could turn any day now. Have you seen pictures of the summit in winter? It's like the North Pole. There'll be frost two feet thick on this building."

"What about the backcountry huts that aren't quite so high? Madison Spring?"

"They all get snowed in by Thanksgiving. No way out except by ski or snowmobile. No electricity."

"I think electricity's going to be hard to come by for a while."

"Listen, where do you live?"

"Boston."

"Get yourselves back to Boston before things get any crazier. At least then you'll be at home base. I've got a mother with a bad hip in Bangor, and I know there's a roof and helpful neighbors there when it gets cold. Electricity or not."

She might be right, he thought. Home base instead of a gamble on the mountains.

"All I know is, I want to be in my own house right now," she said. "Not out here in the wild."

A door slammed behind them and they both turned to look. Paul walked in, crossed the room, and sat down at their table. He looked exhausted yet miles from any rest.

"Paul!" Jane said. "Are you hurt?" Others noticed his entrance and watched him closely. A few began to approach the table.

Paul shook his head and unshouldered his backpack as he swung his other leg over the bench. Mud ran up to his knee. He pointed to the half-eaten bowl of chili. "Can I have this?" he said, picking it up and beginning to eat. Jane and Doug exchanged a look. He bent to his work and finished the bowl in four large bites, gripping the spoon like a tool. His hands were filthy. As Paul washed down his supper, Doug watched his Adam's apple bob. Paul set the water bottle on the table with a rattle and closed his eyes, suddenly motionless, shrinking into himself. He winced against some unseen pain.

"Paul?" Jane asked quietly.

"It's all gone to hell down there," he said.

"What has?"

"Everything. You name it."

"Phones? Lights?" said Doug.

"Neither. The whole government's missing in action. My brother is dead."

"Oh, no," said Jane.

"I drove down to Concord. That place is upside down. No power, stores ransacked. You'd hear gunfire at least once an hour. Jeremy is police captain. Was. They said he tried to stop looters at a bar. His body was still there. I buried him."

"Jesus," said Doug.

"I don't know where Sarah and the boys are," Paul said.

"Did they leave a note?" asked Jane.

"No note."

"Concord is, what, fifty thousand?" said Doug. "Big enough to mean trouble for the cities farther south."

"Were you able to find out anything about what's happened?"

"They're saying it's an attack on our grid. Whatever they did worked because it knocked out everything. The only way to get information is on AM/FM radios, the emergency broadcast network. People who have battery radios or hand crankers can get it. There was one down the street. I listened while I dug. Same three-minute message over and over again. Curfew at six o'clock every night. Martial law. National Guard mobilized in state capitals. Price freezes. Banks closed to prevent runs. It's bananas."

"How did this happen?" Jane said, almost to herself.

"One of the interns at the north visitor center seems to know about computers. He was talking about something called zero-days. It's like a glitch in software that has no patch. He went on and on, I didn't really understand it. But one thing he said that I could follow is that our government has a hundred people working on offensive cyber operations for every person working on cyber defense. He said people have been predicting an attack like this for years."

Doug and Jane exchanged a glance as Paul took another long drink from his water bottle.

"And then something strange happened." Paul shook his head. "I returned by way of Route 25 instead of the interstate. Just to see what else I could find. I stopped in Moultonborough—the town with that little fixed-wing airstrip?" He sounded dazed and was practically talking to himself. "I must have gone up and down every road and checked in every business on Main Street. Knocked on doors, called out until I was hoarse. There was nobody there. Not one soul."

THREE

The hiking party left before dawn. The Danish family would form part of their number. Before they set out, Ove and Doug exchanged contact information and established a series of steps to reach each other in the days and weeks ahead. Ove and Linda hoped to cross the border as soon as that evening. They would drive straight north the moment they reached their car and not stop until they entered Canada. Ove said he would leave word for Doug at the crossing if possible, and certainly at the Danish consulate in Montreal. They also developed ways to find each other once more if the family could not leave the United States and decided to return to the mountains. The flare they would paint on trees, rocks, and other prominent points would be the Danish flag, a white cross on a red backdrop.

An air of urgent preparation filled the cafeteria space from four a.m. onward. The cooking staff made oatmeal and coffee before packing up their own things. Hikers secured tents, rolled up sleeping bags, and cinched stuff sacks, pulling everything tight and bringing out their coldest weather layers. Gear had tended to spread even in the short amount of time they had encamped at the observatory. Pulling everything down tight and making it fit became an effort, and the space buzzed with the energy of a hive. Although the vast majority were leaving, there was an attempt to remain quiet in deference to those few who slept on, and so the travelers spoke in whispers. Several of the remaining party joined the assembled hikers in the hallway as they received final instructions from Paul and Jane away from the cafeteria. Doug and Tim stood nearby watching, wrapped in their warmest jackets against the morning chill. Doug drank coffee, and because there was no cocoa, he gave Tim a mug of it as well just to hold, to warm his small hands. He attempted one sip and made a horrified scowl against its bitter taste, even cut with milk. Jane briefed the group, advising of the timeframe for their hike, their likely rest points, the hazardous parts of the ravine, and the plan upon their arrival at the trailhead.

Jane made her way to Doug. She quietly told him they had confirmed by radio that cars seemed to be unharmed in the trailhead parking lots. He asked if she would look in on his and gave its description.

"Will you be here if we come back up?" she asked.

"Depends on when you get back up," he said, smiling. "If not here, then look for us at Madison Spring."

"Good choice. It has the biggest pantry. But don't stay longer than a few weeks or you'll get snowed in." She smiled and winked at Tim, said "Hey!" with a friendly grab at his midsection, and turned to go. Switching on her headlamp, she proceeded toward the front of the group. Paul was there as well and was shouldering his way into a large backpack. The two rangers were formidable in their mountain attire. They looked ready to attack a glacier.

The leave-taking was hard. Each member of the two families embraced the other. After hugging Linda and Ove, Doug held them each at an arm's remove and took a moment to study their faces, imprinting the memory in case he did not see them again. He had said goodbye before to friends met in the mountains, but never at a moment of such intensity. "*Man må gøre en dyd af nødvendigheden.* One must make a virtue out of necessity," Linda said to him with her old twinkle, briefly cradling his cheek in her hand. "Make the most of this time with your son. Take care of each other. He is very lucky to have you." Ove told Doug that he would pray for him and his boy and looked forward to welcoming them to his home in Copenhagen one day. He smiled in his good-natured way, and Doug knew it was how he would remember his new friend. The children parted awkwardly, in a gangly enfolding of limbs. Both adults and particularly Linda were very gentle with Tim. Doug noticed that the boy, in mimicry of the adults' manner of embrace, patted the backs of each person who took him into their arms. He was not giving comfort, Doug realized. Instead, he was simply performing what he understood to be the basic mechanics of the action. At the sight of this innocent pantomime Doug's heart gave way and he turned his face from the others.

Fierce wind blew in as the doors opened and the large group filed out into the dark. Doug and Tim sheltered around the corner of the hallway behind a glass partition. The sky was clear, but the air was cold, in the twenties at most. The wind bit with a sharp reminder of their precarious place on the mountaintop and the absolute necessity of their shelter. The sun had not reached the many peaks below them, which lay wreathed in starlight. Mountains stood in relief like negative space, each sharp and featureless apex laid out before the next. Doug took Tim's hand, and they stood together watching. The trekkers filed away mutely in the darkness, their headlamps evenly spaced in a line directed toward the vestiges of an unknown civilization. Like a party of torchbearers facing the void. The cold and empty air enveloped them at last.

***

"Why didn't we go with Viggo and Sofia?" Tim asked as they sat at a cafeteria table. The space felt much bigger with so few people in it. There were only seven others. It was quiet in the manner of a house at midmorning after everyone has left for the day.

"It was time for Viggo and Sofia to go back home, buddy. Back to Denmark."

"But we could have hiked down the mountain with them today."

Doug hesitated. As usual, the boy had found his way to his father's weak spot. He had just been thinking the same thing. "Well, their car is parked in a different parking lot than ours. The parking lots are really far apart."

"Isn't there a bus?"

Doug felt himself being pinned down. He did not want to lie, but he didn't know how much he was ready to reveal yet either. A year earlier he would have already redirected the conversation. But Tim was a year smarter and less easily put off. Doug kept answering one question at a time, limiting himself to what was asked, determined not to say more than necessary.

"Yes, there's a bus."

"Couldn't we have taken the bus to our car?"

"I suppose."

"Well, why didn't we do that?"

"If we'd done that, our hike would have been over."

"I think I'm ready for our hike to be over," Tim said with a sigh.

"Are you, pal?"

"Yeah. Will we be done soon?"

"We're going to stay up in the mountains a bit longer, buddy."

"How much longer?"

"Not sure."

"Are we sleeping here again tonight?"

"Yep."

"Can I move my sleeping bag to the corner where Viggo and Sofia's dad slept last night?"

"Sure. Why do you want that corner?"

"Just has the best lighting, I think. For reading."

"No problem."

"Dad?"

"Yeah, pal?"

"Last night, did you see if there were any more fires?"

"I didn't see any more fires last night."

"And did you see if any trees were on fire?"

"No trees on fire. But we're still going to stay up here until we know it's safe."

"OK."

***

They passed the day exploring the observatory inside and out. The suddenly vacant space felt unnatural and foreign, like an office building on a weekend. As they examined each new area, Doug tried to keep his mood light but felt the gnaw of indecision. They were so alone. He realized how he had come to rely on his new friends and longed for their company. Above all, he questioned the decision not to hike out with them. Linda had practically begged for him to come along. But if regret at not leaving pursued him, the compulsion to remain in safety for his boy had won out. For the moment it felt safer here, away from unrest and discord. He would take it day by day—hour by hour if needs be.

In the afternoon the wind died down and the sun burned clear, making for fine conditions outside in a jacket and hat. The boulder field of the summit was as pleasant as it had been hostile the day before. The sublime vistas lightened their moods. Views of the country spread to each point of the compass. Tim enjoyed hearing what was in each direction—the sea to the east, Appalachia to the south—and strained to see these things even though they were well beyond the reach of his view. They took sightings for the hiking party using a pair of binoculars they had found inside. Doug knew that their route had taken them out of the field of vision as they made their way around the mountainside. Gusts of wind blew with sudden violence and produced nervous laughter between them. They both felt the power of the place where they strangely found themselves.

Inside, they explored the observatory. They had spent the previous day shuttling between their small room and the cafeteria, but the building was large and repaid wandering. It had two floors. The lower floor contained supply rooms, storage space, a large industrial-grade pantry with walk-in refrigerators filled with food, as well as cold-weather equipment such as shovels, ropes, boots, and ice axes. There was a museum exhibit focused on the summit's extraordinarily harsh weather. It listed wind speed records and featured interactive displays on atmosphere and storms. They made their way to the lighthouse-like turret that stood as the highest inhabitable structure on the summit. It was part of the museum tour and featured a recreation of an alpine weather observatory at midcentury. There were crude instruments and dials, dusty leather books, gray wool socks hung on a guyline, and an old-fashioned telephone box. The windows were too small to command much of a view compared to the scene outside. Other weather station facilities in the compound were more modern and authentically scientific. These seemed to be off-limits to tourists and visitors, but several doors had been left ajar in the rush to evacuate. Large computers, presumably there to collect and analyze atmospheric data for the entire Northeast, stood dark. There were workstations for five or six scientists, laid out in a modern and comfortable space. Knobs and displays revealing pressure, temperature, wind, and other indicators lined one wall like the bridge of a ship. Double pairs of exterior doors closed and sealed firmly. At each entryway they found dressing stations with parkas, heavy boots, and ski goggles hung and ready for use. Shovels and crowbars also dangled neatly by the exits.

Several other hikers walked around the summit as well, but the cafeteria remained the point of gathering. A certain torpor that Doug preferred to avoid attached itself to that space. One or two trekkers passed the afternoon napping, giving the impression of despair. There was no more arguing or tension, but a type of resignation filled the room, which remained in semidarkness and had begun to give off a stale aroma of unwashed people and overworn clothing. Most of the others who had remained did not appear to have done so intentionally, like Doug, as a safer alternative to the world below. Instead, several of them seemed to be in a sort of stasis or holding pattern. Others appeared to have lost the willpower to make any decision at all. There was a sense of an inability to cope with events of such magnitude and gravity. Doug surveyed those who lingered on. A Spanish couple in their early sixties was there, haggard about the face as they tidied and re-tidied their things. The man in the orange socks whom Tim disliked had stayed behind and was zipped into his sleeping bag, snoring. A group of three young women practiced yoga exercises in oblivious and self-important voices. One person who pulled on his heartstrings was a girl who looked younger than twenty. She sat alone and was glued to her phone, even though Doug knew she could not be connected to a net-work. He was clear-eyed about the need to put his family's needs first and did not intend to be distracted by becoming anyone's savior. But something about the girl, who could well have been his daughter, made him decide to check on her. Setting Tim up with coloring in an unoccupied space in one corner of the caf-eteria, he made his way to her table.

"Hi there. Any luck with that thing?" he asked.

She looked up, startled. "Hi?" she said in a surprisingly high voice.

"I'm Doug. My son over there is Tim," he said, gesturing.

She seemed to relax slightly. "Sarah. I've seen you two to-gether. He's a cute kid."

"He had no idea he'd be stuck this long on a hiking trip with his dad. He agreed to five days, not a minute longer."

She laughed. She looked like a college freshman: nominally an adult, but still childlike, with unlined skin, large eyes, and teeth that were yet too big for her head. Her long dark hair curled down over her shoulders, and she retained the hands and fingers of a girl. Her short, chipped nails had been painted in the colors of a rainbow. She looked uncertain. He thought of Tim alone at that age in a place like this.

"Decided not to hike down with the others this morning, huh?" Doug said.

"No, I just—I have one more day backpacking on my itinerary and then I was going to get picked up at the trailhead tomorrow afternoon. So I figured I'd just wait it out up here and then hike out tomorrow."

"Beats pitching a tent in a parking lot."

"Right."

"Who's picking you up, if you don't mind my asking? Is it someone reliable?"

"Oh. Yeah, it's my brother. He'll be there."

"He lives around here?"

"He goes to Middlebury, in Vermont? It's like two and a half hours away."

"You go to school too?" He opened a package of orange peanut butter crackers and began eating, offering them to her as well. She took one and gestured with it as she spoke.

"I'm taking a gap year. I graduated in May and was going to start college next fall. Not sure what will happen now."

"Kind of a curveball, I guess."

She gave a bitter little laugh. "This hiking trip was supposed to be the kickoff of my big year of adventure. I was going to go to South America next month, see Argentina, see Chile. Have a year traveling and practicing Spanish. Spend the South American summer down there. *Find myself*—whatever. The other day, I was trying to contact my airline to see if I could adjust my flights without getting charged. Then the Wi-Fi cut out. I keep trying to get back on, but it just—" She started to retreat back into her phone.

Doug looked at her. She was very young. He spoke gently. "That sounds like a cool trip." When she kept looking at her phone, he continued. "You know, I think one way forward right now is not to try to think too far ahead. You spend all afternoon worrying about a flight and then the Wi-Fi cuts out. Or the flight gets canceled because all flights are grounded for the week. And they rebook you. Or not. Or you worry about whether you should hike out of here, and then a storm blows in and keeps you on the mountain anyway. Or a car shows up and drives you down. Suddenly all that worry is wasted."

"So what are you saying, just take it easy and don't stress? I'm not sure I'm that easygoing."

"No, me neither. We're all stressed. I'm stressed too. I'm just saying there's a lot that's out of our control right now."

"I keep refreshing my phone, restarting it, recharging it, hoping the Wi-Fi will come back on. Just trying to check all my feeds, to see if there's any news, any word from my friends. I'm totally obsessing."

"Do you mind if I give you a piece of advice? For the rest of the day, try not to think about the trip to South America. Don't think about college next fall. If you catch yourself, redirect your thoughts. I'm not saying those things aren't important. I'm just saying there's no point in worrying about them *today*. They're way down the line and you can't do anything about them. You've got more immediate concerns."

She was listening. He continued.

"You have a day on the summit of Mount Washington. How are you going to spend it? At the very least, it's probably the last mountain you'll climb this year, right? So enjoy the view. Breathe the fresh air. Don't waste this day focused on something you can't change. You'll look back and regret it. There's also practical stuff to do today. What do you need to do to get ready to hike out and meet your brother? Do you have enough food for a few days in case he's held up? Are there supplies here at the observatory you want to borrow? Are your water bottles full for tomorrow's hike? Focusing on those things might help take your mind off your trip."

Sarah looked as though she might start to cry, but she nodded in recognition of what he said.

"You and your brother, you have parents anywhere around here?"

"They live in San Diego."

"He's probably been in touch with them. So when you meet up with him tomorrow, he'll tell you how things stand with your folks. And the two of you will have each other."

"Do you think we should try to drive to California?" she asked, wiping her nose.

He did not know what to say. He thought such a journey would be long and dangerous and that he would not want to undertake it with a young child. But he knew nothing about this young woman or her family. He could help her get through a day of uncertainty in the observatory's cafeteria with a short pep talk. But he couldn't chart out her future. He suddenly saw Jane's perspective. Still, he wondered if he might be the only sensible adult she encountered before she and her brother made a fateful decision. He felt responsible.

"I think Middlebury is a safe, quiet, beautiful town. You and your brother could probably stay there and not have any problems while this thing blows over. I also think that a journey to California would be tough, but that there's a lot of value in finding your parents. But hey—this is an example of what we were just talking about."

"Yeah."

"That decision is ten or twenty steps ahead of you. Don't worry about it yet. This problem might be moot by the time you get in a car."

"Moot—I don't know what that means?"

"Maybe you get down the mountain and your parents have come to Vermont. Maybe they're in the car with your brother."

She smiled. "That would be amazing."

"Listen. My boy and I will be around through the time that you leave tomorrow. If you need to talk, or need help packing, or want a thought partner, or anything like that—just let me know."

***

No rangers returned that evening. The man in the orange socks loudly fretted over their arrival and the impending darkness. He had brownish yellow teeth and bad breath; he smirked even when soothsaying doom. His advice was to withdraw into the backcountry while society collapsed. Some of his comments began to stray in the direction of conspiracy theory, and nothing could have made the idea of a mountain retreat less appealing to Doug. He decided to remove himself and Tim from the cafeteria. He wondered whether he had some obligation to stay and fend off the others from the man's unnerving prophecies. Yet he decided once more, and with a little guilt, that his first duty was to his son. Nor did he invite Sarah or anyone else to join them. He would not have turned her away, but he did not want to be in the business of starting factions.

The kitchen staff had left that morning, so they made themselves a cold dinner from refrigerated cafeteria fare: pretzels, chips, and a candy bar for Tim; cheese and yogurt, and a shrink-wrapped sandwich for Doug. They both drank chocolate milk. Preserving routines as well as his son's teeth, he made sure that the boy brushed carefully after so much junk food and sugar. The sinks in the men's room used motion sensors. Tim delighted in running back and forth between them, trying to keep them all on at once. Afterward, they settled into their room and closed the door against the oppressive chill and long hallways of the darkened observatory. Motion sensors controlled the hallway lights as well and switched off suddenly, plunging the space into gloom. They had found a chessboard in the cafeteria and brought it with them. He hoped that these domestic rituals would insulate the boy from fear and doubt.

It was an anxious time. He found himself preoccupied with what to do the next day. His body ached from the hike to the observatory, and he felt low in spirits. Whenever his son asked him a question it felt like an interruption from his own thoughts, and he had to be startled out of a place of uncertain reflection.

"Dad?"

"Mmm."

"*Dad!*"

"What?!"

"You're not paying attention!"

"I'm thinking, Tim. I can't talk every minute."

"You've hardly said anything since dinner!"

"Take it easy on your dad. I'm doing my best."

"Well, it's your move. I said check."

"OK, I'll go." He had to stop himself from making an aggressive play for the boy's queen. His instinct was to strike back when lashed, the same as anyone. He tried to maintain the balance he had struck between offering competition and destroying the boy's spirits with loss after loss. At all events, the damage was done, and Tim was now upset with him.

When the boy was angry or hurt, he displayed several tells as clear as a cardplayer signaling a partner. He puffed out his lips and slumped his shoulders. He averted his gaze and refused to meet his father's eyes. Sometimes he hid behind a door or around a corner. This behavior could last for moments but rarely as long as hours. Doug tried to coax him out of it with entreaties and reason, but in these moods the boy was a universe of negativity and defeatism. "You'll probably just never listen to anything I say again!" he declared. It took effort not to respond to such an overreaction. To grow defensive or even to laugh aloud at the sheer disproportionality of it. His own level of fatigue and patience usually dictated his response. Or his level of physical pain. If his back throbbed, or his knee, or if he had a headache, he could find himself growing peevish and begin to sulk himself. Carol had helped him recognize this. Often, he found that he resented the boy's outbursts well past the point at which Tim's own mood had recovered. This created an odd dynamic in which the child, recognizing his father's foul humor, instinctively played a sunny caricature of himself to try to lighten the room, the child being father to the man. The effect was cloying and obnoxious, and it made Doug want to escape. In their former lives, they could go to their separate spaces and regroup. Now there was nowhere to go. He couldn't abandon his son, even for a few moments of fresh air to recharge. He was all the boy had.

He realized that he was not following his own advice, so confidently given just a few hours ago. Instead of enjoying an evening of safety and comfort, he was dwelling on decisions that were several steps ahead and well outside his control. Matters that might well be mooted out by events. He needed to wait until the morning and see where things stood. Paul or Jane might return. The weather could shift. The Wi-Fi might switch back on. He checked his phone's signal for the tenth time that evening. News could arrive from another hiker or party heading to the summit. Anything could happen. What mattered was to rest well, stick together, and keep positive. He apologized for his moodiness, resigned the chess game, and offered a thumb-wrestling tournament. Soon they were laughing again. The air in the room began to lighten.

***

Sarah hiked out the following morning, followed by the yoga group. As she prepared to leave, Doug noticed that she had been buttonholed by the man in the orange socks. He was standing too close and seemed to be pressing his ideas onto her. Doug could only see the man's back but read discomfort in the girl's face. She was avoiding eye contact and speaking little. It was plain that she did not want the man's attention. He decided to step in and ease her out of the situation. As he approached, he watched the man reach out a long hand with surprisingly thin fingers and grasp the girl's upper arm. He did so in the familiar manner with which old men had been casually handling young women all their lives.

"Morning. Heading out?"

They both started and turned. The man removed his hand. As he looked at Doug, he still wore the patronizing smirk that he had presented to the girl. His mouth a rictus of mischief. Doug faced him for a moment before directing his attention to Sarah.

"It looks like you're about to go. If you've got a minute, I wanted to go over a couple things about the trail before you set out. Can we chat?"

Relief flooded her face. "Sure. I was just leaving."

The man scowled and walked away, muttering.

"You OK?" Doug asked after watching the man retreat to his little encampment.

"Fine. He's just creepy. You don't think he'd follow me, do you?"

"Did you tell him which path you're taking?"

"No."

"Good. I think you'll be fine. Just keep your head about you and be aware of your surroundings. Mind where you camp. I get the sense he's staying put."

Doug saw that she was well prepared. She thanked him for his advice the prior evening, and for his concern. She looked ready for the day ahead and eager to begin.

"If your brother isn't there, you can always hike back up here," he said to her paternally. "Leave a note for him pinned to the trailhead bulletin board. He might even be able to drive up, if he's got a good car and the road is clear."

"Will do," she smiled and shifted her weight. Doug realized she was not quite ready to leave. "What will you and your son do?"

"We're working on that."

"Do you need a ride someplace?"

"Thanks. But you guys are going west and we're east. We're from Boston."

"I didn't even ask you about your situation yesterday."

"Don't sweat that. It's the job of old people to worry about young people, not the other way around. You'll see one day."

She smiled a lovely smile. He saw what she must have looked like at Tim's age. He hoped she found her parents.

"We might stay up here for a while. Go to one of the cabins. Enjoy the quiet. We're aiming for Madison Spring if you need to find us."

"That sounds nice." She paused once more. "I was wondering if I could ask you—has anything like this ever happened before? Like in your lifetime?"

The question was very innocent. He understood that she viewed him as an old man. As all children viewed all adults. *In your lifetime*—the words conjured a black-and-white image of a midcentury kitchen with a linoleum floor and a coffeepot from Sears. He answered her on her own terms, but with a light touch. "Not that I can remember. But I was able to manage growing up without Wi-Fi."

She smiled. This non-answer seemed to reassure her. "Take care," she said. She turned and left, hiking into gray weather. The clouds were the color of pencil lead and looked like they might hold snow. Her breath became cold smoke.

***

The Madison Spring Hut, where they had first met their Danish friends, was a day-hike away due north. Because Mount

Washington was the highest point in the national forest, it was mostly downhill or flat walking above the tree line. Avoiding several detours to the summits along the way, they could keep the hike moderate and make good time. They packed their things and prepared to set out before the weather fouled. Since he had already mentioned to Jane that they might go to Madison, he felt no need to leave word. And he didn't particularly want the remaining trekkers second-guessing his decision or deciding to join them. It was time to part ways with the observatory and its scattered occupants. They would see whether Madison could offer practicable shelter for a few weeks. It was more secluded, lower, and therefore safer than the observatory. But there was no way to know until they visited and saw for themselves.

They ate a large breakfast. Afterward, he scavenged as much food and as many supplies as he could fit into an empty duffel bag that he found in one of the weather labs. Madison might be well outfitted, but there was plenty here that they could put to good use. The cold weather at altitude would preserve perishable food, which they could eat through in the order of its expiration. First the shrink-wrapped sandwiches, then the milk, then the yogurt; save the commercially packaged cheeses and finally salamis and jerky for last. Candy bars and chips would keep for years on end. Not that it would come to that. Surveying the kitchen, he took note of industrial-grade canisters of staples like peanut butter and mayonnaise, salad dressing and flour. He picked up a ten-pound jar of peanut butter as well as a fifty-count package of hot dogs. He told himself that there was no harm in being overprepared. Packing carefully so as not to smash the food or rupture containers, he stacked products of like type into small cardboard boxes, which he then laid carefully next to one another in the duffel. There were also a flashlight and batteries, and a larger and better-quality first aid kit than the compact backpacking kit he kept in his pack. He took two pairs of ski goggles and two heavy pairs of leather gloves. As for fuel, he would have to rely on what he found at Madison or else make a return visit. After careful consideration, he took a CB radio and charger from an equipment rack. He switched both to the same channel, plugged in the counterpart, and placed it on the table in the room that he and Tim had shared. Who knew if Paul, Jane, Linda, or Ove might stumble upon it, take its meaning, and get in touch.

When full, the duffel bag was cumbersome and heavy, adding another forty pounds at least to his already substantial burden. It would be a hard day's work. Reconsidering, he placed the jar of peanut butter in the bottom of his backpack and moved some clothing into its place in the duffel bag. The difference was marked and eased the strain when he hefted the duffel bag's shoulder strap. They wore their waterproof outer layers so they would not have to stop and change clothing if rain or snow began to fall.

Tim accepted the itinerary without complaint. To him, it was another day on a backpacking trip with his father. He remembered the Madison hut and had a fond association with it because he had liked the snickerdoodle cookies. "Will that guy with the gray beard be there?" he asked.

Doug had been wondering the same thing. "Not sure. I guess we'll find out."

"I liked him."

"Me too."

"He gave me an extra snickerdoodle."

"He did?"

They left with nothing more than a wave to the Spanish couple as they played backgammon. They were both attractive and lean, and looked as though they could ski all day and drink wine together all evening. He wondered if they had children, and why they would ever leave Europe to vacation in New Hampshire of all places. They seemed in no hurry to go. Perhaps they planned to ride out the next few weeks here on Mount Washington. He did not stop to ask. The man in the orange socks had returned to his sleeping bag, as seemed to be his daytime custom. His thin, curly hair protruded from the top, and his face, as ever, was averted. His glasses sat folded beside his pillow, with their greased lenses and loose hinges. He must certainly be a bachelor: someone's uncle, avoided with distaste at family gatherings. Full of awkward jokes and shady investment opportunities. What life would he return to? Doug tried not to let himself be dissuaded by pity. He fixed his gaze once more on the small beam of light that had become his life's focus. He would protect his son. This was his object and his purpose. He was ready to leave the observatory. It had been the site of hard news, harsh weather, and a sad leave-taking from friends. The people who remained were not people he wished to know. He did not want to return to this desolate place.

***

Once they started hiking, they did not look back for some time. The first half hour was hard going. There was no sun to warm their faces, and the wind remained high as they descended. They walked north toward Madison rather than south, the direction from which they had approached the summit with their friends two days earlier. The terrain was rocky and uneven. Doug was never the best route-finder and in the flat light had trouble maintaining the faint trail. Across from them loomed Mount Jefferson. A few sections of loose scree allowed them to glissade downward, skidding four or five feet as their feet sank into the wet pebbles with each step. It was efficient but precarious work, as they teetered on the verge of losing control and falling forward. Tim clearly enjoyed the freedom of the movement and its recklessness. In certain moods at home, he would spin and spin until the point of falling down, leaving to chance whether he cracked into a sharp corner of furniture or a waiting doorjamb. Doug had half a mind to hold onto the boy's collar as they made their way down the mountain. He checked the impulse. They had proceeded several hundred feet safely already and were past the steepest aspect of the face. If he were to fall now, he would tumble harmlessly for a few yards and thereby learn his lesson.

When they watered for the first time and looked upward, their progress surprised them both. They could no longer see the observatory or weather tower, just the end of the incline far above. Fast-moving clouds obscured it in whisps of atmosphere and just as quickly blew away again. The peak had been more prominent from the south: a more symmetrical triangle, with lower shoulders. But it nevertheless loomed impressively above them. They had nearly descended as far as the point on the southern face where Linda and Ove and their children had left them for their summit bid a few days earlier. Doug caught at his son's jacket sleeve and flashed him a smile, which the boy returned wearily.

The tedium of a hike was something that the boy had not

yet fully embraced. He no longer asked repeatedly how much longer they had yet to walk. Doug had broken him of that cussed habit. But it was clear that he viewed the walking itself as a kind of ordeal to be borne, rather than the very purpose of the venture. He looked forward to being done for the day, eating special treats, staying up past his bedtime, and the anticipation and memory of the trip more than the actual foot-to-foot business of it. He mostly kept his head down as he walked, saying little, except in rare voluble moods early in the day. At those times, his exuberance overmatched all considerations and he leapt and bounded like a mountain animal. But his current register seemed to be a mild withdrawal. He was not surly, exactly, but seemed intent on concentrating and getting through the work as quickly as possible. It was unclear whether he was tired or anxious. Doug was learning not to overtax him with conversation as they hiked. Instead, he took pleasure in the companionable silence, retreated into his own thoughts, and enjoyed the view.

The trail was well-marked, with frequent signposts giving both altitude and mileage. The summit ridges offered a warren of trails. Arrows pointed the way to the Madison Spring Hut. Additional signs with prominent insignia identified which sections of the route overlapped with the Appalachian Trail, which spanned thousands of miles along the country's eastern seaboard from Maine to Georgia. They skipped optional summit detours up Mounts Jefferson and Adams, skirting around both peaks and remaining within view of the tree line. The wind blew fiercely near each exposed summit as they passed beneath it. Doug kept an eye on the world below but could see little because of the cloud cover, which enveloped the trees and lower mountains in haze. He sensed a stretch of valley to the west but could not see it clearly. He also scanned the various paths as far as his eyes could follow them. But throughout the day's hike they saw no other traveler. In this vast expanse of wilderness they were alone.

Doug's extra bag was heavy and difficult to manage. His back ached as he strapped the large duffel over alternating shoulders. Tim gamely offered to carry it for a stretch but soon realized that it was beyond his ability. The bag was nearly the weight of his own person. As a result, they made short, frequent stops throughout the day where it could be set down briefly or re-adjusted. Doug tried every permutation of carriage, including wearing the duffel's two hand straps around his arms with the bag against his chest as a sort of inverted backpack. Nothing remained comfortable for long. He despaired of the condition of the food, so carefully stowed, and whether it was being ruined or smashed with each readjustment. The sandwiches in particular could not survive such discombobulation. Sweating freely, he stripped down to a long-sleeve base layer. The exertion wakened his appetite, and they snacked throughout the day, taking in trail mix and energy bars at each stop as well as during the march. They did not make a long lunch break. At a certain point, Doug simply wanted to reach the final hut and set down the duffel bag once and for all. They began their descent down the upper flanks of Mount Adams into the high saddle between that peak and Mount Madison, where the Madison Spring campus lay sheltered. As the trail wrapped around the mountainside, the familiar cabin came into view below them. They cheered with weak relief, Tim having adopted his father's spirit of exhaustion despite his own far more modest burden. Smoke curled upward from the hut's chimney.

Doug descended the final quarter mile gingerly and in some pain. His knee and back ached, and one of his toenails seemed to be loosening and threatening to give way. There was nothing to do but complete the march. As they made their way down toward the cabin, he scanned the area. He could see no other backpackers sitting out at the picnic table, or other signs of life beyond the chimney smoke. When they reached the cabin at last, they saw no one. At this lower elevation the air was cool but windless. They set down their things outside on the picnic table with groans. Doug breathed a sigh of relief when the door to the hut was unlocked. They walked in, not stopping to remove their boots. The main room stood empty and silent. Doug had half expected to see David sitting on his perch, an elfin sentinel unfazed by the onset of war. But David was not there, and the stool itself had been removed. Doug called hello but heard no answer. Yet a fire blazed in the hearth. They walked from room to room, starting in the dormitory, where the beds were all stripped with no backpacks or sleeping bags in sight. The dormitory felt cold compared to the main room. In the kitchen, which was adjacent to the main room, there were more recent signs of activity. A small pot on the gas range held a portion of soup. Perhaps it was waiting to be heated.

"Dad, look!" said Tim. An aluminum sheet stood next to the small gas oven with two rolled balls of cookie dough on them, ready to be baked. They were cool to the touch. "Snickerdoodles!" Tim said. To him, it meant cookies. To Doug, it meant they were not alone.

"Let's go around back and find the place where the hut warden stays," said Doug. "I think David is still here. This looks like his dinner."

Exiting the hut through a door at the back of the kitchen, they walked across a short, open-aired, covered walkway to the door of the hut warden's humble lodgings. Doug tapped at it and said hello. There was no answer. The handle was not locked. He called again as he entered.

The space contained the quarters of an ascetic. Everything was tidy and well organized. Doug envisioned David sweeping it daily with some rustic Tibetan broom of bundled zebrawood. Two pairs of shoes were placed neatly by the door. The front room had a table to the left with a darkened computer, modem, radio, and other communications equipment. The workspace was stacked with pencils, papers, and topographic maps. To the right was a bookshelf that contained volumes on local flora and fauna, the Appalachian Trail, as well as texts on eastern philosophy and geometry, a history of Rome, works by Shakespeare, and classic novels by writers like Tolstoy, Austen, and Dickens. On the floor, a small electric heater sat unplugged. Beyond this simple living space lay a sort of bedroom, with a single bunk in the same style as those found in the dormitory. It was dressed with sheets and thick wool blankets rather than the sleeping bags of traveling hikers, and it had been made neatly. A three-row, open-style bookstand held David's plain clothing. On the bedside table was a glass of water and a devotional or prayer book.

They returned to the main room of the hut. "Why don't we set you up here by the fire while I look around for David?" Doug said. "I think he must be off collecting firewood or something."

"No way, I don't want to stay here by myself!" Tim said, alarmed.

"You're not too tired to come with me and walk around a bit, looking for him?"

"Can we sit here for a few minutes first and have a snack?"

"Good idea. Let's have a snack."

***

While they ate, the late afternoon began to descend upon the mountain's saddle. Unlike so many other sections of the Presidential Traverse that were wide open to the elements, this area, despite its elevation, offered a sense of shelter and protection. The hut was situated in between two large peaks, Mount Adams to the south and Mount Madison to the north. This placement frustrated the unbroken vistas that they had experienced on the summit of Mount Washington, which provided tremendous views but also left a feeling of exposure. The hut was also nestled down into the lowest point of the saddle, obscured from some angles by low scrub brush. Although the trees did not grow high at this very upper limit of the timberline, there still was enough vegetation to break up the monotony of the barren rock that they had hiked through all day. It was not possible here to see horizon in every direction. Or to be seen.

The sound of a tinkling bell, of the type a shepherd would place around the neck of livestock, reached them at the table. Tim heard it first; his every sense was keener than his father's. Doug frowned. They had seen no sheep or goats at any point in their travels. The only animals were squirrels and birds. They rose, put on their jackets, and went outside.

David approached them with a surprised expression on his face. He wore a bell on a leather thong around his neck. It was the type one might find adorning Swiss cattle, and the anachronism suited him. He balanced two large bladders of water on a pole across his shoulders and walked unsteadily under the weight. Doug raised a hand in greeting. Grimacing with the effort, David leaned to one side in a practiced but graceless motion and unburdened first one, and then the other water bladder so that they remained upright on the picnic table and did not spill. He was perspiring and sighed after the effort of carrying so much. If he had come from the river, it would have been a quarter-mile walk, most of it uphill.

"Hello, David. We met a few days ago—Doug, and this is my son Tim. We stayed here at the hut? You checked us in and showed us around."

David looked at them, confused and catching his breath. He fanned himself with his hat for a moment before answering. "Hello again. Nice to see you both. Do you have a reservation for tonight? I've been closing the hut down for the season."

"Maybe we could talk about it inside," Doug said, glancing down at Tim meaningfully. "Let me help you with that water."

***

They sat at the table in the main room closest to the door, where the air was cool. Both men had exerted themselves and remained overheated. Doug set Tim up to play at the other end of the room before the fire. He was out of earshot but well within view. Before long, he was making explosion and zooming noises as he played with his spaceship and gave voice to its adventures. Both men drank from their water bottles.

"You're welcome to stay here tonight," David said quietly. "I'm planning to close up tomorrow."

"What if I told you we'd like to stay a little longer?" Doug said.

David thought a moment. "I'm leaving in the morning. I suppose if you're still here when I leave it's not the end of the world. Considering."

"We don't want to be any trouble, and we're happy to pay. I just want to keep my boy safe."

"I can understand that. How long do you have in mind?"

"Not sure. I'd like to see how things play out below. Stay up here a few days, maybe a week. Maybe longer."

David looked at him mildly, with an inscrutable expression between surprise and amusement. As he did so, Doug studied the asymmetry of his beard and prepared to make his case. But David only sighed and said, "I've thought of staying myself."

Doug felt a flood of relief. He unclenched his jaw and slowly exhaled. "Why don't you?"

"I've got a daughter in Burlington. I'm going to try to get to her." He stopped and shook his head at some unseen antagonist. "Frankly, I don't know if it's the right decision."

"How old is she?"

"She's thirty-one. She has a family, daughters. She doesn't need me. I guess I need somewhere to go, to be honest." He smiled awkwardly. Some of his Zen assurance was beginning to fade away now that he actually began speaking.

"It's a time to be with our children," offered Doug.

"I do feel that way."

"Burlington is a couple hours' drive?"

"I don't have a very fast car, so I usually take more like three. But it's not so far."

"Can you make it on one tank of gas?"

"Oh, certainly."

"Have you been down from here since . . . since the surge?"

"No. I was going to go down a few days ago but then the rangers told us to stay put. Help organize things and find all the hikers. So I've just gotten the radio reports. And what I read on the computer. We can get Wi-Fi up here but it's very slow. Could get Wi-Fi."

"Any cellular service?"

"Used to be, if you stood over near the wood chop. But not anymore."

"I don't suppose you saved those computer articles."

"Sorry. I'm not very good with that sort of thing. I generally get the newspaper in print. When I'm not up here."

"What was the latest news?"

"Seems like the cities are falling apart. Lot of looting, rioting. Curfews. That worries me less than what I hear about whole towns emptying out. People will be fools and take what they can from each other. I'd expect that. But when they disappear altogether . . ." He shook his head in wonder. "I don't know what's going on down there."

"I heard about that too." Doug paused a moment, and they sat in silence. "Burlington is a quiet town. Reasonable place to wait this out."

"Yes. Yes." David studied the grain of the wooden table. It was easier to talk about logistics. "They've got a spare bedroom on the first floor. That's where they usually put me. It's out of the way. I don't think I'll be much trouble. I can help with the girls. Help with the cooking." He was talking as much to himself as to Doug. "I don't know how long all this will last."

They both gazed out the window. In these new circumstances, David seemed less like a seer or an oracle than a lost old man. Heavy lines surrounded his eyes like tributaries. His

liver-spotted hands were thick at the joints and trembled ever
so slightly. The silver beard that had appeared so lustrous from
a dozen paces looked overgrown up close. He had reached the
point in life where some men begin second-guessing decisions
rather than proceeding with confidence. Waiting for others to
step forward. Prone to sentimentality and watering eyes. Fretful.
Uncertain. Worrying a callous with an anxious thumb. Sleeping on a problem, then sleeping on it again. Not wanting to
be a burden. Needing to get back. Calamity was a young man's
game. He had much less life before him than Doug, but it was
his own, and now he had to safeguard it. Perhaps for the first
time. It was an awful thing, trying not to be forgotten. Doug
hated to see it.

They sat together for a few moments. Finally, Doug said,
"David. How long can my son and I stay here safely? Is there
enough food? Will it be too cold? What's the point of no return?"

Without removing his gaze from the window, David smiled
for the first time. "Come on. There are some things I need to
show you."

***

They began in the storeroom off the kitchen. It was uninsu-
lated and naturally chilly, like a walk-in refrigerator. Doug felt
relief as they stepped inside. Neatly stacked from floor to ceiling stood enough provisions to last several months, if rationed
carefully. There were canned tomatoes, corn, pears, and peaches;
four jars of marinara and arrabbiata sauce; powdered milk canisters; several bags of flour, sugar, and dry pasta; tins of yeast
and salt; butter, lard, and oil; a few canned soups, stews, and

chilis; crackers, cookies, granola bars, and oatmeal; and even tea, coffee, and energy drink mixes. There were egg substitutes and a dozen bottles of wine. Doug smiled ruefully to see a large jar of peanut butter of the type he had so painstakingly hauled from the Mount Washington observatory.

"We have backpackers bring their own food, as you know," David said, with his upturned hands on his hips. "But several times each season we do a full-board weekend for yuppies. People in their fifties and sixties who get outside rarely and expect to eat well on vacation. We close the huts to everybody else. It always books up six months in advance and is a cash cow for the Appalachian Mountain Club. We charge about triple what you paid and serve breakfast and dinner. Pretty nice meals, actually—flapjacks, cinnamon rolls, lasagna, baked bread, fruit cobbler. We can't always use fresh produce, so many of the ingredients are canned. And those last longer, too. We can get pretty inventive."

"How do you get this food up here? This stuff must weigh tons."

"One can at a time. The kids who work as hut wardens always load up their packs when they come up. We always have supplies coming up and trash going down. They never travel empty-handed. It's well organized. And there's an ATV that can handle the northwest trail out of Madison. I can't carry as much on foot, so I load that up and drive up the heaviest supplies: wine bottles and other liquids. In the spring Paul brings his horse and packs it down for a few trips. Some things they haul up the cog railway to Mount Washington and then hike over to here. We manage alright."

"And then you just always have a store of food like this?"

"Not at all. You have very good timing. Somebody over-ordered for our last full-board group of the season. This was two weeks ago. So we have more food left over than we otherwise would. Anyhow, we always make sure the hut has some provisions for winter, just in case."

"Skiers?"

"Yes, backcountry skiers use the huts as shelters. There's an honor system that lets them take what they need as long as they leave some cash behind. And there's food for the hut wardens to eat during shoulder seasons, when there aren't any guests."

"Have you got the recipe for those snickerdoodles? My son has been talking about them all week."

David smiled once more. "That'll be in the kitchen. This way." Tim had joined them and followed behind, listening.

David explained the mechanics of the gas stove, including replacing its propane tank outside and cleaning its connection points. There were extra hoses, coiled and shrink-wrapped, if any of the ones currently in use failed. The pilot light was a perennial headache and David showed him how to start the oven manually without it. The gas ranges were an easier discussion, as Doug had used them already as a guest. But David walked him through the common problems that both devices encountered, and how to fix them with the hut's tool set. Elsewhere in the kitchen, the crude wastewater system needed no further explaining. There was a cold-weather dumping point closer to the hut than the one the guests had used. David said Doug would thank him when the temperature dropped.

They stopped and looked at each other. Both had begun talking as though Doug and Tim would be staying much longer than a few days. Doug thought that might well be true. They might leave by the weekend. But it made sense to learn as much as he could about the campus in case they tried to winter over.

"You do need to know what you're getting into when it comes to weather," David said.

"World's worst weather, we read all about it on Mount Washington."

David looked serious. "They clocked the wind speed up there at 231 miles an hour. That's a class-five hurricane. It doesn't get nearly as bad over here as it does up there. But the cold and the storms are extraordinary. Well below zero. Once you pass the first good snowfall, you'll be stuck up here. Without a snowmobile, the only way out is to hike, and the snow is just too high. I'll leave you my snowshoes. But you need to watch out before you're committed for longer than you want. Without Wi-Fi, there's no radar, no weather forecast. You don't know when storms are coming. Unless you're careful, you'll be in that cabin for months. You understand that?"

"I understand."

"And consider this. We get a lot of snow even down at the base. From January through March, we've got snowplows running weekly and sometimes daily on the main road through the national forest. I don't know if those will run or not this winter. If you get down there and dig out your car, you might not be able to drive anywhere in it. There might be three feet of snow on the road. You understand *that*?"

"I got it."

"And you still want to do it?"

Doug sighed. He checked to see that Tim had wandered off out of earshot. "Listen, I don't know how long we're going to stay. It might be just a few days. We've both got to make our own choices. I don't want to gainsay yours. But from what I read before it went dark, things are falling apart down there. We live in Boston. I don't feel safe going back until some sort of order is restored. We might get stuck up here, as you say. But that means no one else can *get* up here. So we're at risk from the weather but at least we're safe otherwise. For now, I'll take snow. Pick your poison."

David nodded. "Pick your poison."

"And there's another thing." He hesitated.

"Well?"

"We don't have family to go to, like you. I'm a widower."

David looked down. "I did wonder. That's hard. Hard on both of you."

"There's nobody back in Boston waiting on us. Not much of a home, either. *He's* my home. And I'm his."

***

David showed how the solar generator supplied a small measure of power to the hut warden's apartment and how the solar panel had to be cleaned and repositioned. On cloudy days it would barely generate any energy. Yet one good afternoon of direct sunlight could supply power for ten hours, including the computer, radio, lamp, outlet for charging radios and phones, and even the space heater if used judiciously. The firewood stockpile seemed bountiful to Doug. But David said it would go quickly, and that a good practice would be to haul and chop wood every day and add to the pile. This meant hiking down several hundred yards to where the trees were tall enough to provide lumber. There was a timberfall that David used to find fallen wood, saw manageable logs, and drag them back up for chopping into firewood. A large blue tarp covered the fuel and tied down to an iron ring bolted into the side of the chopping block, and another screwed into a tree stump.

"Keep enough wood inside for a week in case it rains or snows. And don't let that wood out there get wet, or it will be the devil to burn. Bring the axe inside every night. It's a good axe, no sense in letting it rust." Kindling and long matches stood ready in a box of supplies by the fireplace.

"Where should we sleep? Can we use your quarters?"

"You're welcome to my room. But it's starting to get cold in there already. By November it's useless. It's too hard to keep that room warm. See how the walls are thinner than the main building? It was an addition, built much more recently. Wood and plywood rather than stone. Some damn fool cutting corners. The generator isn't strong enough to let you use the space heater for long, and that thing is too old to run safely overnight. If it starts a fire, this whole place could burn down."

"Those dormitories were pretty cold, too."

"Skiers use the dormitories in winter, but that's just for a night or two, and I'm sure they wear every layer they have. You could do that too if you're just going to be a few days."

"Could we set something up in case we stay longer? Helpful to have an extra pair of hands to move any furniture I couldn't carry on my own."

David thought for a moment. "We could bring a couple of beds into the great room, near the fireplace. A good fire will heat that entire room, and you can have one going all the time. I'll help you move the beds."

The work took an hour. The sky outside began to darken as

David and Doug emptied two single bedframes of their mat-
tresses, tilted them sideways, and carried them through the
doors and hallway to the great room. Navigating down the
half-stairway from the lofted dormitory was difficult. The ancient heavy bedsprings seemed forged from the same iron that
made the crampons and axes of the golden age of mountaineering. Tim helped by carrying wool blankets and pillows. They
set up a sleeping area close to the inner wall that separated the
great room from the kitchen. This kept the beds away from
the drafty outer wall comprised mostly of windows and established a bedroom of sorts away from the living area. At Tim's
request they positioned the two beds next to each other, about
three feet apart.

David heated a larger portion of soup and made more cookies, enlisting Tim as his assistant. He showed the boy how to
roll the dough into balls and space them on the baking sheet.
It was thin, each end tilted upward at a forty-five-degree angle,
its surface stained by years of melted butter and sugar. Timing
the cookies' turn and then removing them at the zenith of their
rise was a matter of utmost seriousness to their host. He used
the chronograph function of his mechanical watch, removing
it from his wrist and showing Tim how to operate its pusher to
stop and reset the hand at the precise moment. Reacting to his
tone of voice, Tim listened with a grave expression. He understood that David invested concentration and discipline in the
task and that these labors yielded comfort as well as nourishment. It was simple work, but good in a fundamental way. The
word that occurred to Doug as he watched the old man and
the boy together was *grace*. A heartening aroma began to fill the
great room. This brought a large smile to Tim's face, all freckles

and teeth, which in turn produced a mild one on David's. In his wisdom he had learned to appreciate a thing quietly. They laid three settings at the table closest to the fire, dressing it first with a red-checkered tablecloth and mismatched candles. Darkness enveloped the hut. From afar, the gleam of these domestic rituals between men of three generations shone out into the night, penetrating dimly in the void but casting a warm glow.

They ate companionably. There was no great abundance of laughter, but both Doug and Tim enjoyed the camaraderie. Tim, in particular, took to the company of this avuncular figure. David asked Tim about his favorite subjects in school, and soon the two of them were engaged in a discussion of the White Star Line, whose most famous ship had been the *Titanic*. It became clear that David had no particular interest in that vessel but was well-read and had a mind for facts. He quizzed Tim on the date of the ship's sinking, the definitions of port, starboard, bow, and stern, and the *Titanic*'s last port of call before setting sail through the North Atlantic. Tim was uninterested in the soup, a beef broth, although Doug persuaded him to try a few bites in light of their status as guests. Doug prepared peanut butter crackers for him, as well as a string cheese that they had brought from Mount Washington. He noticed that David ate slowly. He dipped his crust of bread and closed his eyes as he chewed each bite in gratitude for another day lived in health and good humor on the mountainside. Their dessert was rich and warm, the taste of butter strong after the simple soup. It was a fine meal.

Afterward, David excused himself to his hut and soon returned carrying a bottle of Scotch and two glasses. He wore a sly grin. "I usually have a nip to celebrate the end of the season," he said, pouring a measure for himself and one for Doug. "I keep the bottle behind Hawthorne on my bookshelf. You're welcome to it."

"Can I go play?" Tim asked.

"You go ahead," Doug said. "Clear your plate." After doing so, Tim skipped over toward the fire, as lighthearted as Doug had seen him in days.

"Sure you won't stay a little longer?" Doug asked.

David smiled ruefully as he eased himself back into his chair. "No. I belong with mine just as you belong with yours. I'll be alright. Nobody's going to bother an old hippie in a Volkswagen."

"What can I do to help you pack up?"

"Let's leave it for the morning."

"Fair enough."

They sat and drank the whiskey.

"You'll enjoy the sunsets. If you stay on. I haven't spent too many late-season nights up here, but the few I have . . . When all the peaks are white, the sun just lights them up. Orange and pink. It feels like the roof of the world." He smiled. "What a show."

They handled their glasses, coating them with the viscous amber liquor and watching it play against the candlelight.

"Thank you for all you've done for us," Doug said. "We've enjoyed your company. I know Timmy has."

David nodded. "It's my pleasure. He's a fine boy. And you're a good father. I think you'll do well here. Nice to leave the hut in your hands."

Doug raised his glass. "To the future," he said.

"To today," David said.

They drank.

FOUR

In the morning, Doug helped David load up his ATV well beyond any sensible capacity. Items dangled from either side of it like some Himalayan rickshaw. David even planned to pack out a large bag of garbage, strapped low to the back of the vehicle. He wore his own large backpack and several layers of clothes that wouldn't fit into it as he prepared to step on and ride out. His knitted mittens were enormous. A helmet and goggles completed the ludicrous costume. Doug tried to talk sense into him.

"You'll never get down with all this. There's twice as much packed on here as you can carry."

David smiled. "Son, I've made this trip dozens of times. Maybe a hundred. I always pack this much."

"But won't some of it fall off? How do you manage the rough sections of trail?"

"Slow and steady. There's one piece of trail where I usually have to unpack and repack, but I don't mind. That's why I'm leaving early. Quit your fussing. Tim? Come here a minute. I have something for you." He removed his goggles as the boy stepped over. David reached into his jacket pocket and carefully extracted something. He handed Tim the wristwatch they had used to time their baking the previous evening. "I want you to have this. You remember how long we bake the snickerdoodles?"

"Yes."

"Tell me."

"Six minutes, turn, then four and a half more minutes."

"And how big is each dough ball?"

"The size of a reindeer nose," Tim said without hesitation.

"That's right. Teach your dad." He winked. "That watch is special, Tim. Take good care of it and wind it every day. I wore it for thirty years. Now it's time for someone else to have it. When you're a little older, it will fit your wrist and you can wear it too. Until then, use it to make cookies and time other things."

"Like what?"

"Like how long it takes the sun to rise from behind that false summit there to the top peak there," he said, pointing southeast. "Especially over the next month."

"How long?"

"You'll have to let me know."

Tim smiled at the game. "Thank you very much. It was nice to meet you."

"You're most welcome. I enjoyed meeting you too. Good luck, Doug," he said, shaking hands. "I've got your letters to your friends, and I'll mail them the first chance I get. Your people will know you two are safe and where you are."

"I appreciate it. And you'll radio back up when you get the chance."

"I will. I'll look around a bit, find some news, and get you an update. Might take a few days."

"We're not in a hurry."

"Well, goodbye. Hope to see you again."

"I hope so, too. Be safe."

He drove away slowly, the very picture of a bygone time. They watched him perched on his mount like an old rascal riding a tricycle in a grainy photograph. Once more Doug and Tim were alone.

Tim sighed loudly. "I liked David," he said.

"Me too."

"I wish he could stay."

"Me too."

"Did you ask him to stay?"

"Yes. Twice. But he wants to be with his daughter, and his granddaughters. And we can't hold that against him."

"OK. I guess not."

They watched David drive down the trail and out of sight. Doug kept expecting parcels or bags to fall from his vehicle.

"Well, we'd better make an inventory," Doug said. He wanted to keep their spirits up with some sort of project.

"What's an inventory?"

"It's a list."

"A list *of*?"

"Of all the food in that storeroom. Let's go—I need your help."

***

That task occupied them for an hour. This was the limit of the boy's attention span for anything other than movies and video games. They found a grid-style notebook of the type used for geometric equations or technical sketching. Tim counted out the containers of each type of food and reported them to his father, who recorded them carefully in a neat hand, using tally marks. This would help him organize the cooking, create some sort of schedule to maintain variety, and keep an eye on dwindling supplies. The boy's habit was to find a food that he liked and eat it obsessively until he could no longer stand it. He had once spent a year beginning every day with a cereal bar until, one morning, he refused to touch one. Now the foodstuff was like the memory of a grade level in school not to be repeated. His father hoped to avoid such a problem by rotating the supplies of their pantry. After they recorded everything, he read back each provision and the boy checked it against what he saw on the shelves before him. He seemed to like being an equal partner in the enterprise and his father intentionally made several errors which his son corrected with importance. They also worked up a game of combining the names of two items to make a ridiculous neologism. Milk and juice was *moose*. Granola and Nilla wafers was *granilla*. Flour and pasta was *flasta*. Tim had the makings of a wordsmith and delighted in manipulating language. Soon they were giggling.

This work made them hungry, and they ate an eclectic-tasting lunch from the larder they had just inventoried. As they ate, Doug capitalized on the good mood to deliver news that he hoped would not cause too much discord.

"Today we'll start having quiet time after lunch."

"Why?"

"Because we might be here for a few weeks, and quiet time is good for both of us. It's part of our routine."

"But what can I do during quiet time? I don't have any toys here."

"You can play with your spaceship. We can look for books that you might like to read on David's bookshelf. You can take a rest. And you can explore—inside or outside."

"Can I go anywhere I want?"

"You have to stay in the clearing if you go outside—that means anyplace where I can see you. But that gives you a lot to work with."

"OK."

"If you do go exploring outside, you have to take the whistle."

"Why?"

"So I know if something's wrong. Anything happens and you need me, you blow it and keep blowing it until I show up. Got it?"

"What would happen?"

"Well, if you fall and hurt yourself, or you get lost, or you see an animal or something."

"What kind of animal?"

"David said that there are black bears in these mountains. We need to be very careful about them right now."

"Why?"

"Because they're going to be hibernating soon, where they rest all winter. And what do bears do before they hibernate?"

"Eat."

"Right. They eat. They won't eat *us*. Black bears are not like big grizzly bears you've seen in books. They're smaller. What they like to eat around here is berries and acorns. But they're still dangerous. If you see one, I want to know about it right away."

"What do I do if I see one?"

"If you're with me, tell me. If you're by yourself, look to see if it's a grown-up or a baby bear, which is called a cub. If it's a cub, or if it's a grown-up with a cub, it's very dangerous."

"Because parents protect their babies."

"That's right."

"But why would just a cub be dangerous?"

"It wouldn't. But parent bears don't let their cubs go far on their own. So if you see a cub, its mom is nearby."

"OK. Why not its dad?"

"Well, that's not really the way bears do things."

"So it would be the mom."

"Right. Now, a grown-up bear on its own without a cub is less dangerous."

"OK."

"But all bears are dangerous."

"*Dad.*"

"Sorry. This part is important, so pay attention. If you see a bear, make sure it knows you're there. Bears don't like being surprised. So make noise. Not really loud or sudden. Don't yell and scream but talk to the bear. *I see you, bear. I don't want any trouble. I'm just going on my way, Mr. Bear, Mr. Bear—I'll just mosey on out of your neighborhood.*"

"Dad!" He was laughing.

"And then you sort of back away. Slowly. You don't turn and run. Bears look fat and slow but they're actually much faster than we are."

"Because they're quadrupeds."

"How much?"

"Dad, quadrupeds. It's a word. It means they walk on four legs."

"I knew that. Anyway, if you run, it might chase you."

"Well, I could outrun a bear."

"No. This isn't a game. You're a very fast boy. Maybe even the fastest. But it's like saying a bike could outrun a car. The slowest car is faster than the fastest bike. Same thing with a bear."

"Well, I think I could beat a car on my bike."

He knew his message would sink in and that to press the point would only create obstinacy. "So what you do is, while you talk to it—*hey-o Mr. Bear*—you just back away. Make eye contact with the bear so it knows you see it. And blow your whistle like I taught you."

"How will you stop the bear?"

"We won't need to stop it. The bear will see that you aren't a threat and will lose interest."

"But what if it doesn't lose interest? Can you stop a bear?"

"David showed me that there is a rifle here."

"A *gun*?"

"Yes, a gun. We don't want to use it, but we'll protect ourselves. From bears or anything else."

Tim was impressed. He was quiet for a moment. Then he said, "Do you think there are any books about bears in David's room?"

"I think there might be. Let's go look. *After* we clean up our dishes."

***

There were several books on the shelf that they could read together. Doug made note of *The Adventures of Tom Sawyer* and *Adventures of Huckleberry Finn* by Mark Twain. There was *Treasure Island* by Robert Louis Stevenson and *The Call of the Wild* by Jack London. The two volumes he pulled out for immediate reading together were *The Lord of the Rings* by J. R. R. Tolkien and *Watership Down* by Richard Adams. Both books seemed filled with enough adventure and childlike fantasy to keep the boy's interest and were written at a suitable level. They could alternate reading aloud to each other. Doug wanted to keep up Tim's strong literacy skills during this time. For himself, he pulled out several books to consider taking on: *Middlemarch* by George Eliot, *Jane Eyre* by Charlotte Brontë, and *The History of the Decline and Fall of the Roman Empire* by Edward Gibbon in six volumes.

"Plenty of time, uh, for this," he said to himself.

There was something reassuring about the small library's age and constancy. Nothing even remotely contemporary stood on the shelf: nothing to remind him of the failing state of the world below. The Adams was the most current book, and it was over fifty years old. To earn a place here, a volume had to endure for generations. It had to be written of a certain quality and it also had to physically last: not to be a text file or a piece of digital ephemera, but to be a physical object, ink printed on paper bound between boards and secured by a spine. It must be stitched well and kept dry. Few of the volumes were what anyone would call fine editions, but they had been constructed in an age when books and other things were made with craftsmanship. The titles dealt in themes greater than any given moment: not fads or trends but matters as old as humanity itself. He could not imagine David browsing new paperbacks or asking about the latest book club choice. It was no surprise that he was an avid reader, but his bestsellers would span centuries or even eras and would have no notion of fashion. The Gibbon had been written 250 years ago. It described events dating back to the time of Christ.

While Tim spent quiet time inside playing with his spaceship, Doug checked the solar panel and made sure it was clean and correctly positioned. For all its promise of sleek green energy, it was a heavy piece of equipment with rusted bolts and sharp corners. He wiped a coat of grime off its hot surface with a rag and then touched each connection point of the cables that led to the generator. It was a sunny enough day to provide a charge to the computer and radio. He went into the hut, switched them both on, and searched in vain for signals. At intervals he called out to Tim to let him know where he was. He also plugged in the CB radio he had brought from Mount Washington, as well as his cell phone, leaving both on as they charged. Neither was even remotely useful, but there was no harm in being prepared. There was no cell service or Wi-Fi signal. He decided to make these rituals part of his daily routine as long as they remained here. He could give Tim the task of carrying the cell phone around their campus looking for service. Maybe there was a bar to be found in some corner of the hut. Doug decided they would carry the phone to the twin summits of Mounts Adams and Madison, both close enough to touch, to see if the phone worked there.

That afternoon they made a project of scouting and retrieving firewood. They brought the saw, canvas bag, and shoulder harness that David kept hanging by the lumber stack. They wore fleeces and hiked down under the tree line in cool weather. David had indicated generally where the timberfall would be found. Under the canopy, the temperature dropped noticeably. They stepped over fallen pine needles and leaves, keeping sight of the trail leading back to the campus. Tim would excitedly spot wood on the ground, but it would be a rotted-out stump or trunk, decomposing into light compost and useless as fuel. Eventually they found a fallen tree that seemed to have come down that season. Several of its branches had been sawn, and there were piles of darkening sawdust scattered about.

"I'll bet David has gotten logs from this one," Doug said. "I'll saw off this section of trunk, and then we can drag it up to the hut and chop it up into logs."

"But what can I do while you saw it?" Tim asked. He was tired and low in spirits, and his defeatism threatened to take over.

"You're going to help me saw. Come here, I'll teach you."

"I get to use the saw?"

"Just stay away from the pointy end."

It was slow work. Doug made the boy wear the spare pair of leather gloves for safety. But the gloves were too large for his hands and the sawing was too hard for his small muscles and low center of gravity. Soon enough, he wanted to take a break, and Doug completed the task. He fell into the rhythm and enjoyed his exertion, only to be jostled out of it by occasional misalignment of the saw, or its catching on a knob or whorl of bark. Getting through the trunk took less than five minutes, but he was sweating by the time it broke free. He framed the accomplishment as one for them both to share. Tim wanly slapped five with him and they set about putting the log in the harness. It was fiendishly heavy and awkward. As he began to drag it like a plow horse, he realized that the weight was too much to pull up to the hut. Its branches kept catching on stones or shrubbery. He decided to saw off several branches and hand one of them to Tim to drag, at once giving him something to do and lightening his own load. This took additional time and effort, and Tim began to grow impatient as he waited. By the time the two burdens were ready to be hauled, they were both peevish.

They completed the task only after stopping to rest several times. The harness was of an ancient leather make, a thick and creased mahogany hardened into shape by age and sweat. It cut into Doug's shoulders and the weight forced him off balance unless he bore down and pulled with all his strength. Tim pitched the note of his own exertion to match his father's. Even though his branch was a much smaller burden, for him it still represented an evening's fuel. Once they reached the clearing, Doug offered to let Tim drop his branch and said he would come back for it, but the boy displayed his familiar determination to see a thing through. His father at once marveled at his stubbornness and admired his perseverance. They dragged the lumber around to the back of the hut and lay down beside it, panting. Close above them, whisps of cirrus cloud blew past overhead.

"It was like a workout. We should think of it like our daily exercise—we just went to the gym."

"We have to do that every *day*?" Tim asked.

"We'll get smaller logs next time. We'll learn from our mistakes."

They lay on the ground.

"That was really hard," Tim said.

"I know. I'm proud of you for carrying that heavy log all the way up here."

"Why did we have to do that again?"

"The wood is what will keep us warm. We'll burn it in the fireplace. That's the only thing that will heat the hut. And there's no one to get wood for us: we have to get it ourselves."

"Can't we just use the wood that's stacked against the house?"

"We'll use that, but we'll go through it quickly. You'll see. We don't want to run out of wood. Then we'd be cold."

Tim sighed. "You're right." After a moment he said, "Dad? How long are we going to stay here?"

"I'm not sure."

"Why can't we just go home?"

"Well, it isn't safe yet."

"Why not? Are there more fires?"

"The power's still not on."

"Couldn't we just light candles at our house?"

"That's a good idea. But it's not just about lights being off. Boston isn't a very safe place to be right now. No phones, no lights, no school, no work."

"No *school*?"

"Think of it like a vacation."

"How long will school be closed?"

"I wish I knew. We just have to wait and see."

Tim said nothing for a moment, and his father went on, "The best thing for us is to stay up here until things calm down."

"OK. It's hard not knowing how long it will be."

Doug knew that Tim would process this information and ruminate on it in the coming days. "Do you have other questions?"

"No, not right now." He didn't seem too shaken. But he had been listening closely.

"How are your hands? Did you keep the gloves on while you dragged your branch?"

"Yep," he said, taking the leather gloves off. "My hands are kind of sweaty, but they're OK."

"Good. Let's go have a snack. Then we'll chop some of this wood."

"Can I use the axe?"

"Not until you're ten."

***

David's call came the following day. He chose the right moment: the boy was playing outside for quiet time, and Doug had the hut to himself when the radio crackled to life. It was the first electronic contact he'd had with anyone since the surge. For a delirious breath, he thought the power had been restored and that Jane or Paul was calling with organized plans. But then the familiar voice began to speak.

"Madison Spring, this is Lincoln Woods. Madison Spring, this is Lincoln Woods. Doug, are you there? It's David calling."

He grabbed the radio and quickly lowered the volume.

"David, I can hear you loud and clear. This is Doug. Are you safe?"

"Safe and sound. Good journey down."

"Where are you?"

"I'm at the visitor center east of Woodstock. You two getting along alright?"

"Just fine. Very comfortable up here. We gathered firewood and I've been cleaning the solar panels. We've been checking for cell and Wi-Fi service but nothing so far. How about down there?"

"Same here, I'm afraid." There was a delay between transmissions, and in each dead space Doug feared the connection had been lost.

"Have you seen other rangers? Jane or Paul?"

"No, haven't seen them. It's pretty quiet in the national forest. Empty, in fact. I've been to several of the ranger's stations, and I think most everybody has cleared out."

"Copy that."

Pause. "Listen, Doug—you might want to stay up there a while."

Doug said nothing and clutched the radio. "Go ahead."

"I've driven around quite a bit. Not just here but the environs too. Northumberland, Lancaster, Gorham. No power, people hunkered down and armed. These are very small towns, country folks. But it doesn't look good. People are frightened. Some have relatives missing. They won't talk about it. It's confusing."

"Violence?"

"Some signs of it, although the folks I've visited with say it's much worse farther south. The big cities. It sounds like Philadelphia is practically a war zone. The mayor was assassinated."

"Christ. Any news of Boston?"

"Not much, but I gather it's similar. There was strange chatter on one of the radio frequencies. I was just now trying to listen. It kept coming in and out, a lot of static. I couldn't tell you if it was a foreign language or something else altogether. Some sort of signal or code."

Doug sat grimly for a moment, saying nothing. "How about the border with Canada—last I heard they were stopping Americans."

"Completely sealed is the word I got yesterday. No one in or out except Canadian citizens."

"OK."

"Doug, I think you'd be well shot to stay put for now."

"For a few weeks?"

There was silence over the line. Doug spoke again: "I said, hold tight until November? David?"

"Sorry—just was keeping an eye on a car cruising past. First one I've seen. They've gone now. November at least. The things people are talking about down here are food, heat, and security. You've got all those up there."

"Right."

"Unless—"

"Unless what?"

"Well, you could come with me to Burlington."

Doug considered. "That's generous. I don't want to impose on your daughter and her family."

"I get the sense that usual rules of hospitality aren't going to apply for a while. Good people will want to help each other. You don't need to worry about imposing."

It was a tempting offer. They wouldn't face the dangers of the alpine. There would be others to help make decisions, and children for Tim. They wouldn't be alone. Then again, there were the perils of the journey. And Burlington was west. Boston was south. It would be taking them much farther from home.

"David, when are you setting out? Can you give me a little time to think it over?"

"I'll leave tomorrow. Take the night and think on it."

"Can you stay there safely?"

"Yes, it's no problem. I'll radio back at six a.m., and you can let me know what you've decided. Good enough?"

"Alright, be well. Over."

"Over and out."

✳✳✳

He was preoccupied through the evening but said nothing about David's offer to the boy. The moment he opened up any question for decision, Tim voiced a firm opinion and then was hurt if his advice wasn't followed. Yet even when he held strong convictions, they soon faded away. And in any event, this was no matter for a child to decide. Doug mulled over what to do. His thoughts tended to run toward departure. If he looked beyond the risk of the journey, the prospect of breaking their isolation and merging bubbles with another family felt like the relief of an extended hand. Their chances of finding good information about events would be much higher in town than in the wilderness. As well stocked as their mountaintop cabin was, the food would not last forever; Burlington would offer more dynamic opportunities for resupply. It was closer to the border with Canada if they decided to try and leave the country. A famously easy-going town, it seemed less likely to succumb to the sort of civil unrest that had plagued other cities. Still, he hesitated. Safety was all, and each of these windfalls depended on a journey of several hundred miles through an uncertain world. Several hundred miles away from home, with no sure way back. Moreover, while he trusted his instincts about David, he did not know his new friend's daughter or her family. The journey was therefore not the only gamble. Even if, as David had said, he and Tim would be welcome, these might not be the right people to live with indefinitely during a historic crisis. Doug played and replayed these thoughts fretfully, without coming to any clear resolution. He would make up his mind for sure in the morning. But just to be prepared for an early departure, he gathered their things together after the boy was soundly asleep. Hiking out in time to meet David would mean starting early.

He slept fitfully and woke well before the appointed hour. The decision had crystallized as he slept. With the balance of risks so close, what made up his mind was exhaustion with solitude. The two of them were a remarkable pair, but they remained precarious as two legs holding up a stool. The rest was missing. His wife, Tim's mother. For once, they would not have to be alone—alone together. A makeshift family stood waiting. They had been on their own for so long. So. They would leave and join David on his trip to Burlington. It was a close call, but he felt confident in its rightness. He began gathering their few unpacked things. At a few minutes before six, his son remained asleep, so he took the radio outside where it would not wake him. He stood under heavy gray clouds and waited, radio in hand. Yet no call came. Doug tried David over the line but received only static. He waited a few minutes and tried again without success. Tim came outside, noticed his father's preoccupation with the radio, and asked what was going on. Sensing the uncertain nature of their plans and not wanting to commit and then dash his son's expectations, Doug answered in vague terms.

"I just want to make sure I don't miss David before he leaves on his trip. He said he was going to start his drive today and I thought I could speak to him once more first. I haven't used a radio like this much before. I don't want to mess it up."

"Here, let me see it. I'll do it."

"No, buddy, I think I have it set right. Let's just leave it for now."

"Dad, give it here."

"Tim! I've been working on it for the last ten minutes and it's finally working."

"Fine," the boy huffed and walked away, sulking. There was nothing for it. Doug would deal with his hurt impatience later.

It began to rain not long after Tim woke up. The drops were at first sparse but then became insistent. From the window, Doug watched as the ground around the small campus turned into a sloshing wet mess. He held the radio close and listened carefully for any chatter. The heavy drops grew into a steady downpour by eight that morning. By nine, as the storm intensified, he began to fear for David's safety and felt torn over whether to try to find his way to the visitor center to check on him. Perhaps, having made the decision to leave, they should commit to the issue by setting out to find their friend. His thoughts ran to the car that David had mentioned driving past. Anyone could have been in it, including the type of vandals or thugs who were stealing things and setting buildings on fire. Indecision turned to bouts of panic and then to a dull dread as he came to understand that there was no good course of action. Hiking down into danger, in a fierce storm, with his young son was unacceptably risky. Yet leaving an old man in peril on his own left him uneasy. It was an impossible situation. To calm himself, he returned to his first and only purpose and recited it like a mantra: he must protect his son. Even at the cost of sacrificing a friend. If he led his son into danger, he would fail in his most important charge. If he left the boy and went down alone, he might well orphan him in the mountains. He reminded himself how close the decision to leave had been as a way of talking himself into staying. These new risks altered the balance and augured toward remaining after all. He decided to try all the channels on the radio to alert others to David's predicament, but his efforts were met with silence. Tim's sullenness turned to uncertainty as he saw his father's anxiety fester. He too began to fear for the well-being of his new friend.

They waited as the weather continued, unrelenting. It rained without stopping for three days.

***

Doug was not a religious man, but he came to view the storm as a sort of omen. Perhaps nature had intervened to keep them from making a fatal mistake. It had prevented their movement like Arctic ice freezing a ship into place. Now their ticket to Vermont seemed to have expired. The radio's battery ran out of life, and there was no way to contact David except by hiking down the mountain. Staying began to seem like their best course. That, after all, was what David had said before he made the offer of Burlington. Doug told himself that the old man's sudden disappearance was nothing more than a radio malfunction, rather than a health emergency or an attack by marauders. Or some other pressing need had caused him to leave on his own, ahead of schedule. A voice nagged at him that David would not have simply driven off with Doug's decision to join him still pending. Perhaps his own indecision in the face of the storm had been answer enough for both of them. They could hike down still and try to find their friend—or simply get in their car and begin driving west. But now the safest course seemed to be to stay high, away from whatever was taking place below. The renewed brilliance of the weather at altitude was like a crystallization of their plans. For now, at least, they were staying put.

With the prospect of a longer stay ahead, they began to establish a school routine in the mornings. Organization and habit had often served them well. Leaving the house at a certain time to get to school. The same bedtime each evening, even on weekends. Friday movie nights. Baths every third day. Tim sometimes chafed against so much predictability, but, in general, it helped manage his emotions and allowed Doug to get by as a single parent. His thoughts turned to schooling. At Tim's age, with a second grader's limited needs, Doug did not want to over-emphasize the significance of book learning. There was only so much the boy was missing this fall. His literacy and numeracy were the most important things. Those and his socialization with other children, which for now could not be helped. Doug told himself this as he tried to change the subject of his inner monologue. He felt unsettled about the way they had left things with David. But he needed to do something other than sit and fret.

He did want to ensure that, in addition to fundamental skills, Tim retained the habit of learning and continued to build his ability for sustaining concentration and acquiring knowledge. Although much of a second-grade school day was comprised of breaks, play, and silly time, there were still elements of the curriculum worth developing. He decided that they would work on reading skills without the boy noticing: in the evenings, for pleasure, taking turns on one of the adventure books he had found in David's library. It would not feel like school. In the mornings, they would spend time on math and writing, as well as two other subjects per day. These would rotate between science, social studies, music, and art. He repurposed an old, faded topographical notebook of Franconia Notch State Park and began keeping a record of their daily learning in it. On each day he attempted to write down a few lines of accomplished business. Each line looked paltry but represented a hard-won accomplishment of purpose over entropy. "10 minutes social studies: African geography." "Arithmetic worksheet: subtraction word problems." He prepared each morning's work the previous evening after the boy had gone to bed and made a weekly schedule so they could anticipate each day's activities. Tim liked him to remain within earshot after his bedtime, although it helped that he not be within sight while the boy settled down and went to sleep. If so, a dozen questions popped into his head and the nighttime routine dragged on interminably. So Doug worked on the lessons at the table where they ate.

All depended on the child's fickle mood, which Doug had not seen before through the peaks and valleys of a school day. On some days, he was eager to begin and went about his lessons cheerfully. On others, he resisted and whined at every step, and for his father to mark down just a few lines in his Franconia journal was an achievement. Often these were a stretch: "colored a Halloween picture" or "discussed foliage." The recording of a snippet of meager pedagogy rather than the work itself became the goal. They began punctually at nine o'clock with the Pledge of Allegiance. This was not because of a desire to instill patriotic values. Instead, Doug found that the formal action of reciting the Pledge, which had started each day of the child's education, seemed to click a switch. Whatever he was doing, if his father began reciting the Pledge, he would stop, stand up, place his right hand over his heart, and recite along. At the end, after "with liberty and justice for all," Tim would chirp, "Have a great day!" This, he explained, was what the assistant principal at his school would always say immediately after leading the Pledge. The boy repeated it without a hint of irony.

They used a dedicated table for their daily schoolwork and did not use this space for meals or other purposes. It was away from their living area and the fireplace, in the middle of the set of tables. Tim liked to get up and wander, so they would take five- or ten-minute breaks between subjects. It was an open question whether the time and effort required to refocus the boy after these interruptions was worth their benefit, but at any rate, he was unable to keep still for more than thirty minutes at a stretch. His body was like a coiled spring whose energy must be released periodically. If he was in a recalcitrant mood, he had to be dragged through the work, one problem at a time, like a headstrong mule on a lead. Here Doug confronted the natural resentment bred by one family member pedantically instructing another. It was like trying to teach a spouse to play golf. Whatever the quality of teaching or perfection of tone, the very nature of the enterprise bred annoyance and resentment. Tim would occasionally strike a defiant posture and seek to disprove anything his father said. Lake Baikal was the deepest freshwater lake in the world? Well, what about Lake Superior? George Washington was the first president? Well, what about Abraham Lincoln? Doug's patience was a muscle that grew stronger with time. During the initial lessons in October, it was weak indeed. First daily, then only occasionally, he would have to call a halt to their efforts and announce a retreat to their separate corners, for an exercise break or a snack.

On other days the boy found his way into the flow of learning and could be infinitely curious and bright. Doug marveled to watch his mind work at close range and began to realize how little he had observed this before. The cliché was that children's brains were like sponges, soaking up information. The better analogy, he came to believe, was that brains were like computers, and children had newer and faster machines than adults. When he got stuck finding a word or recalling a fact, the boy could think more quickly and make connections nimbly. He didn't need to have things repeated to him four or five times before he retained them. He was particularly good at remembering character names in stories. If he was in the right frame of mind, he liked to work autonomously on one of the worksheets his father prepared. This nascent habit of independence was as promising as any subject-matter learning. Doug encouraged it by giving the boy space. He would get up to prepare food in the kitchen, close enough to answer questions if needed. The worksheets ranged from rows of simple addition and subtraction equations to analogies to fill-in-the-blanks to reading comprehension exercises in topics like science and history. If superheroes, body humor, or fast cars could be worked into the lesson, Tim relished in the work, completed it quickly, and asked for more. Here Doug observed one of his own weaknesses at play, revealed by the inevitable logic of genetics. The boy had a habit of moving too quickly, wanting to complete a task to earn his free time sooner, and failing to check over what he had done. It yielded rushed handwriting and overlooked nuances. Sometimes he would miss the entire back of a two-page exercise and be charmingly unaware when directed to complete the other side.

The end of a learning session late in the morning produced a mixture of elation and relief for them both. Whatever followed, they had gotten through another day of school. The most unpleasant business was done, and they celebrated with lunch and then usually a walk before quiet time. In fine weather they would test themselves by going to the summit of Mount

Adams, which commanded the best view of the national forest to the south, including the Mount Washington summit. If it was clear, they could faintly see the observatory by using binoculars. Doug had not yet seen any movement or signs of life there, although it was too far to say for sure. He could not trust his eyes at such a distance. Tim had perfect uncorrected vision, but Doug did not want to trigger questions by asking the boy to be his scout for this purpose. The boy's surefootedness in the outdoors began to grow, and he led the trail to the summit with confidence and strength. They better knew how to dress for an excursion of a few hours: what they must never forget and what they did not need. The small daypack with binoculars, first aid kit, water, food, and rainproof jackets always came with them. Both carried whistles. Doug thought about whether to carry the rifle but decided that, as they were the only people for miles, it was probably more a danger than protection.

They began to dedicate their afternoons to tasks around the campus. If they did not need to gather wood, they would chop and store it, clean the solar panel and generator, check for Wi-Fi and cellular signals, repair a broken hinge or door handle, count their food stores, clean their living space, set traps for mice in the dormitory, or cook their dinner. Whenever possible, Doug included Tim in these activities, unless the boy had a mind to spend his time in solitary play or exploration. He did not always care to participate but wanted to know where his father would be and how long he would be there. Once he had this information, he affected a casual disinterest. Yet Doug could see that being alone caused him anxiety. If his independence was growing academically, it was waning in other ways. His father supposed this was natural enough. They were the only two people on this mountain and the child had no one but his parent. To be without him for any reason was to be alone. The anxiety grew particularly acute in the evenings. The boy would not go to the outhouse by himself in darkness. And if Doug had to leave the great room or still less the hut for any reason after Tim had gone to bed, the boy could panic. Although he was a good sleeper, he had awoken once or twice to find the hut empty as his father used the facilities. Once Doug had returned to find the boy sobbing. He said he had called but that his father did not hear him.

Another day, as they finished their chopping, Tim fell into an expansive mood and discussed their new surroundings.

"I like it here. It's like our own house in the mountains."

"I'm glad. What do you like best?"

"Well, school is much shorter. I get to play outside more."

"And what do you like least?"

"I miss my friends. And I wish there was a playground with monkey bars."

"I miss my friends too. I think what I like best is all the time we get to spend together here."

"Me too. We've been together, just us, for like three months now!"

"Well, I'd say more like three weeks."

"You know what I mean."

"I do. So you feel OK about staying a while?"

"Yep. As long as we're not going to move here forever."

***

The first heavy snow came on the third of November. Before then, they had experienced several days of intermittent flurries and even snowfall that had accumulated an inch or two. But then came a period of sunshine and mild temperatures for nearly a week. The weather felt like August and kept them outside in shirtsleeves, lulling them both into a false confidence in autumn's impossible permanence. It also allowed Doug to gently pass responsibility onto the elements for the decision of whether to stay or leave. He knew the wind would soon turn and that they would lose their chance to retreat. But while the sun shone, he chose to let himself believe these halcyon days might continue. In the end, nature decided for them. One morning the barometer outside the kitchen window began to fall by the minute. When he checked it again while preparing lunch, he realized they faced an imminent storm. Dense cloud cover began moving in from the northwest, pushed by high winds. The snow started falling shortly after noon. As they stepped outside for their customary walk, the wind forced them to reconsider. It had taken on a harsher note, altogether more serious than what they had experienced to date. Each gust was backed by another: blow and blow, tearing at their hair and screaming in their ears. The temperature had plummeted twenty degrees since breakfast. They hurriedly brought in laundry that had been set out to dry on a climbing rope rigged between the picnic table and the hut's deck. Tim chased his favorite pants that had come free of the line and threatened to blow away altogether. Doug scanned the campus and saw that they had left open two opposing windows in the dormitory to air out the stench of a dead mouse. They rushed around making preparations for a storm that had already arrived. Tim relished the excitement after so much tedium and began performing kung fu moves with accompanying sound effects. He was like a white-eyed dog with its blood up, zooming around the yard.

"We need to bring in firewood and make sure the tarp is tied down tight over the lumber pile!" Doug shouted over the noise of the wind.

"Follow me!" Tim screamed back in heroic mode. He led a sprint around the side of the hut, nearly falling once but landing like a ninja and turning the stumble into part of his action-packed narrative. They set up an assembly line with Tim in the entryway carrying in logs one at a time from the stack that Doug hurriedly placed there. He tried to estimate while he worked. Conservatively, they brought in enough wood to last them a week of continuous burning. They stacked it on either side of the fireplace. Then he brought in the axe and tied down the tarp tightly over the lumber pile. His hands were bare and quickly became red and raw in the cold. The corners of the tarp flapped violently as he worked to secure it. He remembered seeing a snow shovel near where David had parked the ATV, so he retrieved that and brought it in. Clearing a pathway to the outhouses would not be easy over such uneven terrain, but the shovel would at least allow them to get to and from the privy without stumbling through two feet of snow. He cast his mind over the various implements in the shed to determine whether there was some sort of chamber pot they could use during the worst of the gale.

The hut's roof was sloped enough that they would not have to worry about shoveling snow off it to ease weight. In New England, some homes' roofs caved in under the pressure of feet of wet snow. But the solar panel would need to be kept clean. It would not generate a charge during the storm, when the sky looked like the inside of a Ping-Pong ball. Doug worried that letting snow build up on it and freeze could interfere with its electronics or render it useless for weeks to come. It preserved their one connection to the outside world. The panel was supposed to be waterproof, its wiring housed underneath, sheltered from the elements. He nevertheless placed the broom by the back door of the kitchen as a reminder to clear off accumulated snow daily. He also decided to unplug the computer, radio, and space heater in case there was some sort of short-out from all the precipitation. The last thing they could handle in a blizzard was a fire.

After an hour of work, the snow had painted the ground and the hut's roof white. Doug's stubble and eyebrows were similarly coated, and he looked like Father Christmas. They retreated inside, closed the doors and windows, and built up the hearth. The storm raged. Fickle swirls of flakes whirled and dove in concert like flocks of white birds. Wind howled into the upper reaches of the chimney, occasionally fanning the flames. The storm's arrival was both exhilarating and frightening. They shrank from its power. Both felt suddenly alone and on their own. Doug's mind raced with all that could go wrong: a blocked chimney meant freezing to death. A malfunction with the ranges or gas oven would deprive them of vital hot food and drink. One of them could be lost in the tempest on the short walk to the outhouse. They found themselves unsure of what to do, with more pent-up energy but nowhere to direct it. To keep occupied, they pursued a project Doug had considered but always put off: stitching together wool blankets, end on end, to make a sort of curtain to bisect the great room. This would trap the heat of the fireplace and make for a cozier parlor. Now that the cold had arrived, there was no sense in sitting in a large, drafty room when they could make themselves a smaller, warmer one.

They gathered blankets from the dormitory and used heavy gauge thread from a hiking repair kit meant for patching tents. Wind rattled the windows as Doug taught his son how to sew. They would use the rings and laundry lines already bolted into the ceiling to drape the curtain when it was ready.

The storm darkened the cabin as it passed over the mountain range and blew all around them. Out the windows that ringed the great room, they could see snow swirling but little else. The vortex even obscured the outhouses. Their autumnal New England cabin had suddenly taken on hints of the Arctic. At one point, the wind startled them both by slamming open a screen door, which Doug then secured shut. As he did so, the air temperature startled him, having plummeted further still. When they had grown tired of sewing blankets, he boiled water. They could drink cocoa as they watched the storm. He also used cooking oil and the gas range to pop popcorn, which he sprinkled with salt. Tim's excitement had given way to a look of apprehension as the afternoon wore on. Dark circles appeared under his eyes, and he spoke little. As a special treat, Doug proposed that they read *Watership Down* early that day instead of waiting for the evening as usual. Tim preferred to listen instead of taking his turn reading and huddled close to his father under a blanket. The story spoke of the green pastures of England and the rabbits who lived there. Doug gave voice to each character: timid Fiver, strong Bigwig, and brave Hazel, who led the group from their doomed warren to a new home. Sweetgrass, clean air, friendship, and, above all, courage filled the small hut as man and boy waited for the storm to pass.

***

The next morning's sunshine revealed a frozen new world. Sky and ground shone bright and crystalline in shockingly cold air. Doug guessed that well over a foot of snow had fallen: fifteen inches at least. He framed his estimate less in terms of the urban experience of shoveling a driveway or clearing off a car, and more from his memories of alpine skiing in the mountains of the west. In this place, mere inches were no longer the right unit of measurement. The wind had formed dunes of snow, some as high as four feet, making approximation difficult. They had a hard job even opening the front door and getting outside. The brilliant glare from the sun caused them both to retrieve sunglasses from their backpacks, unused until now but vital if they hoped to spend any time outdoors in such conditions. The wind had died, and all clouds were gone. It was a bluebird day, all traces of menace left behind. They were committed to the mountain now. As they stepped out, Doug reached down, formed a snowball, and hit Tim in the chest with it.

"Hey!" the boy said, instantly plotting his retaliation. Soon they had covered the campus with their footprints as they ran and laughed, breaking the tension of the past twelve hours. In some places, the snow reached all the way to Tim's waist, and he had to force his way through it like a beachgoer wading into surf. They made snow angels and stomped out words with their footprints. Doug switched into big brother mode and began tackling the boy at the hips, which caused him to howl in delight. No amount of roughhousing was enough, and they played and chased until they panted. They spent an hour making a snowman. Without traditional attire they had to improvise his garments, eventually fitting him out as a backpacker. He wore a stocking cap instead of a stovepipe hat, had sunglasses instead of buttons for eyes, and featured an orange tube of toothpaste for a nose.

"We'll call him Gus," Tim declared.

As the boy searched for branches for Gus's arms, Doug began shoveling walkways around the campus. Hut to out-houses, perimeter of hut, wood-splitting area, water-collection point, wastewater dump. There was no even ground to shovel down to. Soon enough he inverted the tool and used it as a level, dragging it behind him to clear away roughly half of the snow and create a path for easier walking. There was no need to clear all the way down to the bare ground. It was much easier than bending and scooping. He shoveled properly on the wooden platform of the four outhouse bays, pushing the snow off the smooth, even surface. His back began to ache in protest of the work, reminding him of the snowblower he had used the past five winters in Boston. Carol had brought it home one day. She had taken such loving care of him, especially when he failed to take care of himself. Tim wasn't able to contribute to the shov-eling, losing focus quickly and making more of a mess than anything. He delighted in the wonderland and played happily while his father worked. At least the weather looked clear and did not threaten to dump on them further that day. The peaks of Mounts Adams and Madison shone above them in splendor with their fresh coat of white. Wind high above them carried whisps of spindrift off the mountains into the sky.

"Hey!" Tim said. "It's past nine o'clock. We need to start school."

Doug made a quick decision. "You know what? Today is a holiday. No school."

"What holiday is it?"

"It's Columbus Day."

"No school on Columbus Day?"

"Nope. Day off! No school!"

Tim ran around in victory as Doug shoveled and reflected on the white lie he had told. He didn't have the strength to teach lessons after the stress of the storm and all the shoveling. Yet precedent was all. If he had declared a snow day, Tim would have demanded one after each subsequent snow. Or they would have had to negotiate how much snow was enough to warrant canceling school. This was a ridiculous prospect when school was held in their home, with no need for travel in the elements. If he had spoken his mind and said, "Let's take today off," that would have likewise opened the door to bargaining from the boy on days when he just didn't feel like learning. Tim had a phenomenal memory when it came to preserving his interests. "But you said" were the words that began many of their most intractable arguments. Columbus Day was a minor holiday that was forgotten as soon as it passed. Tim did not remember when it occurred—just that it was the occasion for a day off from school sometime in fall and did not come with candy or presents.

"I wish we could go sledding," Tim said.

"Who says we can't?"

"*Dad*, you need a sled if you want to go sledding?"

"We've got this," Doug said, holding up his instrument. It was a short-handled shovel with a large, capacious blade, the type carried in the backs of pickup trucks for spreading salt. Either of them could easily sit in it. Perhaps both.

"How do we sled in that?"

"You sit in it like this," Doug said, showing how to sit and hold the handle in front.

Tim looked intrigued. "You think we can?" he said. "Let's try that hill up there."

✳✳✳

We are dug in. Snow never seems real until you can see it. Especially on a sunny day. I knew this was coming and I suppose I'm glad it's here. T is so excited by the adventure of it all that he doesn't think more than a few moments ahead. But I am constantly thinking of winter, then spring. How long can we stay? How long will the food last? Who else is in these mountains? What is happening below? I still don't know if our country is at war or has been invaded or faces some bizarre threat that I can't even imagine. All I know is that we are safe, and together. For now, that is enough.

✳✳✳

In the weeks after the storm, their stay at the hut became an established fact. Days began to bleed together, marked only by the artificial parameters they created for themselves. Breakfast for dinner on Tuesdays. Extra dessert on Fridays. No school on the weekends. No wood hauling on Saturdays. News of the wider world did not reach them. Whatever Wi-Fi and cellular service covered the hut in normal times failed to reconnect despite daily checks. No hikers or rangers came through: they didn't see another living soul. Doug fretted that the three rangers he had watched leave had never returned. Not that any of them had planned to. As he went about his regular tasks, Doug worried in particular about David and hoped he had made it to Burlington. He also wondered about the people in his life. With a certain detachment, he had watched his universe narrow to one small space and one other person. He thought back to a time of downtown lunches with close friends during busy workweeks. Wearing sharp clothes, made of well-tailored, high-quality fabrics. Stylish and meant to last. At restaurants in Boston's Back Bay and South End: sushi spots and Greek tavernas, Indian buffets and French bistros, appetizers, cocktails, dessert, coffee. Requiring a reservation. Encouraging you to stay awhile. And his friends across the table, knowing him and known by him. Laughing or concerned, engaged or bored, if need be. Perhaps exchanging a birthday gift or even making a toast. Breaking bread, sharing stories. Living life. Helping a lonely man fill a void. All of this comforting, rich, vital—gone. If he had thought during one of those meals that he would soon be deprived of those people and experiences, his heart would have cried out. But the removal had been so unequivocal and accompanied by so much fear and motion that the pain felt muted, like the sound of an explosion heard underwater. Would he get it back, this life he had left behind? Would he pick up where he had left off at some point on the other side of this indeterminate siege? He missed his friends but had no way to contact them, beyond the letters he had asked David to send. They seemed a desultory group now. A college roommate. A favorite colleague from work. The couple who had loved Carol and had faithfully kept up with him over third-wheel evenings even when he tried to beg off. Each day spent without them removed them further from his thoughts. He might yet see them again. His focus and purpose had been so acute in the early weeks of their new life that there had been no time to grieve for what he may have lost. Now it seemed that the time to grieve had passed. He felt nothing.

Tim, on the other hand, missed his friends keenly, but in a diffuse way. What he missed was the role of friends in his life rather than individual persons. He needed to play with other children. He knew the names of every boy and girl in his class at school and was well-liked. There was no particular best friend he pined to see. He seemed to spend a bit of time with one and all. His middle-aged father had only so much energy or imagination for games of tag or hide-and-seek. Doug did his best to straddle the line between being a parent and being a sort of big brother, a peer in fun and games. He would take the boy by the neck, wet a finger, and stick it in his ear. Or make body humor jokes. Or talk in a silly voice and lumber around like a caveman. The child's laugh was his father's greatest intoxicant, and he was willing to make himself a fool to hear it. The love of his only family member. But there were downsides to this type of parenting. While it offered him greater intimacy, it also opened him up to being hurt by a child's caprice. Tim sometimes grew angry with him for no good reason. He was only seven and did not know how to direct his feelings in a mature way. There was nowhere to point his frustration but at his father. If his blood sugar dropped, or he despaired of the tedium of their days, or he simply missed his life as he had known it, he took it out on Doug. And when this occurred, where another parent might have shrugged off the tantrum, Doug took it personally and felt wounded. He knew that he was being oversensitive even while the spat unfolded. But he felt helpless to avoid the hurt. He took pride in governing his temper and declining to shout or even raise his voice in frustration. If the time was right, he attempted to teach the boy how to more productively express his feelings. He said: frustration is part of life, but we shouldn't point it at each other. Yet on other occasions his only recourse was to separate himself from his son for enough time that they could both put aside their anger and start again.

He wrestled with whether to have the boy write letters to people from his life. It could preserve a sense of connection and remind him of those he might see again one day. The letters would form a sort of record, a time capsule that could be stored and saved, and perhaps eventually shared with the addressees. His friends, his teacher, the aunts and uncles he saw once a year. But as Doug weighed the enterprise, he knew that it might also puncture the bubble that he had so carefully created here in the mountains. Not the bubble of physical separation but of emotional safety for his child. Writing to these people would trigger questions about how to mail the letters. How they would be delivered. Why no one was writing back. Whether their people were well. Tim might not know to ask such questions, but they were much on his father's mind. He encouraged the boy to express his feelings in other ways, by writing stories or essays or by coloring pictures. Tim had written an entire series of short books about superheroes earlier in the year, and about the *Titanic* more recently. Maybe another topic would present itself and he could fall into the same habit. These undertakings at least would not expose him to the collapse of the only toehold left to them both, which was the cocoon of isolation.

***

The colder weather and the snow prevented them from taking walks on many afternoons. Doug could use snowshoes, but they did not have a pair that would fit Tim. Doug dragged the shovel behind him to level walking paths into the timberfall and through several of their usual trekking routes. But it was arduous work, and it seemed that only a few days after he finished, a fresh snow would undo his progress. He came to realize that they would need some sort of cold-weather project to keep them occupied when they could not spend their afternoons outside.

After wrestling with the problem for some time, he came upon a solution that was sure to challenge them both. They would build a desk and stool for Tim to use as a school workstation. He often complained that the table was uncomfortable because it was too high from the bench, causing him to have to stretch to reach it. Although sitting on some sort of booster would have fixed this neatly enough, Tim was obstinate and would not accede. But taking his work to one of the easy chairs before the fireplace created its own problems, blurring the line between school and home life. It gave the boy too much freedom to bounce around and avoid studying. A proper workstation would allow him to focus on what he was doing and also separate their daily schoolwork from the rest of their routine. More importantly, building it would give them a project. Doug was no carpenter. He doubted they would be able to fashion anything from wood that would be beautiful. But they could make something functional, and they could learn together while doing it. Having a long-term goal to work toward, and then a payoff to celebrate, would be good for morale. It would keep them from idleness and teach Tim something practical on top of the abstract learning of each morning's lessons. Doug knew that he was also grasping at the idea to avoid his own fear of what was taking place below. And of the difficult decisions he would have to make in spring. Their dwindling food. Whether to stay or go.

What to do if someone else arrived or presented a threat. How they would know when it was safe to leave, if the world remained dark. They could not remain here forever.

Burying his dread, he planned. If he could saw through a wide fallen pine he had noticed and make a clean cross section, he would have his desktop. That cut was the first challenge because they did not have a two-handed saw. It would take skill and luck—and doubtless several failures. Using like principles, they could fashion a simple stool for Tim to sit on with a smaller section of wood. The posture of a seven-year-old never ceased to amaze Doug, and he knew that the boy would not need a chair with a back. This simplified the project considerably. Affixing legs to the stool and the desk was the next issue. Doug had seen an adze among the tools, as well as sandpaper, a hammer, and nails. They could bevel the tips of each leg into balls and fit them into corresponding sockets that they would fashion in the underside of the desktop and stool top. The question was whether to secure them there with glue or to nail them in—and if so, whether a nail would split the wood. He did not know lumber and would have to learn the strength of these makestuffs through trial and error. Perhaps there were screws in the toolkit instead. They had no lacquer to paint the furniture, but if they sanded it thoroughly it would present good workable surfaces for a boy practicing arithmetic and spelling.

At a certain point, he realized that he was letting these cavils become obstacles, rather than what they were: problems to be solved together, and indeed the very purpose of the enterprise. There would be much starting over. They would saw a half dozen cross sections for desktops, and a half dozen more for stool tops. They would experiment with nailing the wood to see how it held up under the stress of iron. They would learn to sand and sculpt the legs into fine smooth joints until they found the best three for the stool and the best four for the desk. As they discarded wood from their experiments, they would use it as fuel for their fireplace. Or perhaps Tim would come up with some ingenious use for it. Maybe they would carve toys or whittle chess pieces. There was no telling.

He turned his thoughts to pitching the idea to the boy. He spotted his chance on a Tuesday evening as they finished reading and prepared for bed. Tim was in exuberant spirits after his favorite dinner of pancakes and had particularly enjoyed that evening's pages from *Watership Down*. The heroes had bravely fought off a group of villainous rabbits, and Tim paraded around the great room performing karate moves and making sound effects.

"Tomorrow we start our big project," Doug said with grand understatement.

"Really? What is the project?" Tim asked in excitement. Doug had picked the right moment.

"We're going to build you a desk."

"My own desk!" Tim shouted and began racing around the room, climbing up and leaping off the tables. He came to a flying halt on his father's midsection, forcing the air from his lungs and laughing irresistibly.

"And your own stool," said Doug.

"Can I decorate the desk?" Tim asked in a tone of urgency.

"Absolutely. It will be your desk. You can decorate it however you want."

"Yay, I get to have a desk!" he cried, running again. He stopped in sudden thought. "But how will we make a desk? Do you know how to do that?"

"We'll use wood from the forest. We'll do it together. In the afternoons."

"They have some tools here. Remember that hammer?"

"And we're going to use them. You're going to learn to use them. We'll make a carpenter out of you yet."

"I just wish I had overalls."

He laughed. "Me too, pal."

"Next we'll make me some overalls!" he cried, all manic energy and wild ideas. Doug smiled to watch him. They had endured so much tedium after so much fear and uncertainty. It had not been an easy fall. This release was unexpected, and it was welcome. It was joyful.

Tim sat down, sighed, and said dreamily, "My very own desk."

"Think you'll be able to sleep tonight?"

"I'll try."

***

What Doug gained in morale, he lost in schoolwork. Tim was so excited to get started that he could barely contain himself. The morning's lessons were all but wasted, and they rushed their lunch. In the afternoon, the weather was cold but clear, and Doug said they could skip quiet time just once to get a jump start on their project. They brought the saw and began their hike down to the tall strand of pine trees. They followed the trail, which was covered in several fewer inches of snow than the surrounding field because he had dragged the shovel there a week earlier. He would have done so again today but they would already have too much to carry on the way back up.

As they walked, they felt the optimism of an earlier time. The boy was eager and breathless, taking three steps for his father's one. He bounded forward and back, heedless of the cold or the wasted energy. He talked ceaselessly, and his pink cheeks played against the white snow and the mist from his laughing breath. Seeing his son overflow with enthusiasm was unexpectedly moving after so many numbing days. Just as their world had been reduced to a narrower scope of people and places, so had their emotional palate. Their range of feelings was now a kaleidoscope of grays rather than a true rainbow. But here was a burst of sudden color, like a pumpkin in a snowfield. With it, life sparkled anew. He allowed himself a moment's satisfied reflection. He was doing a good job. His boy was not only protected but had been given the emotional space to experience joy once more. Who knew if other children still had that luxury. Safekeeping, Doug realized, was not enough. He had to give the boy a childhood. And himself a reprieve. He basked in the moment and enjoyed the day. As they walked, they chattered with possibility—the possibility more important than the plans and dreams themselves. Frost clung to the branches with a delicate beauty as they entered the still forest. There were few animal tracks other than those of rabbit and marmot. They walked with a pleasant cadence. The sound of their boots and their laughter echoed among the trunks.

They found their tree soon enough and set to work. Doug had thought ahead of time to set Tim to scouting branches that could be used for the legs of either the desk or the stool. This way he himself could concentrate on the important task of sawing the desktop. He impressed upon the boy the need for straightness and weight. They would do best if they could find three or four branches from the same trunk to serve together. Tim set to his task with vigor and mainly heeded his father's injunction to stay within view. Doug sawed. He began low down on the trunk an inch above where it had split from the stump. That ravaged wood was unusable anyway, but it would give him practice and allow him to gauge the quality and strength of the timber. It was difficult work and required concentration to keep the cut perfectly straight. But his worst fears did not materialize, and he found that the months of practice sawing logs for firewood gave him some facility with the tool. He had not given any care to making a clean cut before, but he knew how to control the saw, and most importantly, how and when to take breaks and resume the work without it becoming stuck. When he cut through his first disk, he was satisfied to see that, while it was jagged and rough where it had split from the stump, he had cut the other side evenly. Barring one conspicuous notch where he had rested, this could be sanded smooth. Even more heartening was the fine color and even grain of the wood. He could improve on the work, but with a careful next cut, he already had a solid underside for the desk if he needed it. He took a break and looked at the branches Tim had proudly displayed.

Preserving their momentum was more important than making headway on the project or using their time efficiently. Hence while he might have liked to stay and make another two or even three disks while his hands knew the rhythm of the work, he suggested they make just one more and then leave. Tim had gathered enough branches for them to make a project of selecting the very best contenders. There actually were several that might answer. The benefit of his desk and stool was that neither need be very tall. The boy himself did not stand four feet. They selected five branches, and then Tim found a perch to watch his father saw one more disk. This work proceeded as well as the first task. Satisfied and in good spirits, they put down their tools and ate a snack. They packed up their things and began the hike home.

"Do you think Viggo and Sofia and their mom and dad got back to their house by now?" Tim asked.

"I think so. It's a long way. They were going to drive up to Canada and then fly home from there. I'll bet they're back by now."

"How long is the flight?"

"About eight hours."

"You'd have to take a nap on the plane."

"That's true. And it's an overnight flight."

"Those are the worst," the boy said knowingly. "Can we have breakfast for dinner?"

"Great idea. I was thinking the same thing."

They walked on, tired and happy.

The man standing near the cabin door seemed to have just arrived. He was wearing a coat and gloves, and his back was to them as they came into view a hundred yards from the Madison Spring campus. At first, he did not see them. He was tall and vaguely familiar. He had thinning, curly hair and wore large glasses. Doug did not have the best vision and could not place him right away. He knew only that he did not belong.

"It's the man with the orange socks," Tim said quietly.

Something about the way he carried himself was off as he walked around looking at things. It was as though he had lost a shoe lift or was missing cartilage in one knee. He moved with an awkward gait and one of his legs straightened more than it should have. Watching him was vaguely unpleasant. Doug thought quickly. He and Tim had both stopped and were watching the man across a clearing. Smoke rose from the chimney, as they had kept their customary fire going through the morning. They had no laundry out to dry, but there were other unmistakable signs of their occupancy. Footprints in the snow. The shovel next to the door, white ice frozen to its blade. They stood in full view, framed by scrubby brush. At that moment the man turned and saw them. He raised an arm.

"Listen to me, Timmy," Doug said evenly as they began to close the distance to the campus at a measured pace. "I'll do all the talking. Don't say anything unless I ask you something. You might even hear me tell a lie or two. Usually we don't tell lies, and we never lie to each other. But I want to make sure he doesn't try to stay here with us or take anything of ours. You stay near me. If I tell you to do something, do it right away and without asking why. If I say go inside, you go inside. If I say run, you run." He turned and looked at Tim as they walked. The boy's eyes were large, and he looked frightened. "Do you understand me, son?"

"Yes," said Tim in a small voice.

"It's going to be alright. Follow me."

The man stood with his arms at his sides and watched them approach.

FIVE

They walked down and into camp. As they drew close, Doug could see that the man looked unwell in his person. He wore scruffy whisps of beard, and his hands were dirty, smudged as black as spent logs the day after a fire. Doug recognized his clothing and realized that he may not have changed since they had last seen him at the Mount Washington observatory over a month ago. He was wearing his backpack. Doug could not understand how he had come to be at their cabin. It would have been nearly impossible to make the hike with snow, deep in places, coating the mountains above the tree line between Madison Spring and the observatory. Certainly, there would have been no one clearing out hiking paths. They were in wild country now. Yet as he looked back toward Mount Adams, there was an unmistakable trail leading from the south. So he had walked. Doug looked to the man's ankles and saw that he wore no gaiters to keep snow out of his boots. His boots themselves were of poor quality, weekend hikers made of mesh and nubuck, and his pants were wet and snow-crusted from the knee down. He could as well have been dressed for a trip to the supermarket as a traverse in the mountains.

"Hi there," the man said as they approached.

"Afternoon," Doug said.

"You two been out gathering wood?"

"Yes." Doug looked at the man, waiting.

"Let me help you carry that inside."

"That's alright."

Surprise passed over the man's face. He had not expected a wary reception. Perhaps he had not expected to see anyone here.

"Think I'll warm up by your fire. Been out in the cold all morning."

"Timmy, go inside and build up the fire."

"OK."

The man watched the boy walk inside a moment or two longer than Doug liked.

"You don't remember me," the man said.

"I remember you."

"We ate a meal together, you, me, and your boy, months ago, in one of these huts."

"I said I remember."

The man considered. "I've got to say, you've lost some of your friendliness since then."

"A lot has happened since then."

"Well, that's certainly true."

"Do you have any news?

"Haven't heard much. Can't get a signal anywhere. I saw another fire to the east a few weeks back. It burned longer than the first one. Burned for almost two days before it seemed to just go out on its own."

"The last I saw you was at the observatory," Doug said.

"That's right," the man said.

"That where you're coming from?"

"That's where I woke up this morning."

"Anybody else there?"

"Just me."

"When's the last time you saw anyone?"

The man figured. "Oh, it's been five or six weeks. Before Halloween, at any rate."

"Who'd you see?"

"Lot of questions, mister."

"It's been a while since I spoke to anyone."

"Just you and the boy here?"

They looked at one another. Doug thought that the man was at least four inches taller than him, and probably fifty pounds heavier. But it was not muscle. Where the months in the mountains had hardened Doug, strengthening his arms and hands, they had made this man even more indolent. He had probably whiled away the days at the observatory, napping and eating, sampling every sweet in the pantry, leaving containers half full. Cans ajar. Waiting to be spoiled. He was at least fifteen years older than Doug. He looked unhealthy. Ears full of wax, nails too long, teeth brown, breath foul. Every moment Doug spent in his presence augmented the distaste that he instinctively felt. The man was wrong. He had been wrong at dinner, wrong at the observatory with his hand on that girl's arm. Wrong here.

"Who'd I see," the man repeated to himself. "It was those two rangers, man and a woman, they came back to close the place up. After they hiked everybody down off the mountain.

Beautiful woman." He caught Doug's eye and tried to draw him into his lechery. "But like I say, that's been some time ago."

"And you've been living at the observatory since?"

"I have."

"They let you do that?"

"They did."

"How's that been going?"

The man barked a sudden loud laugh. It startled Doug and must have startled Tim inside the hut, for there was the sound of something falling and hitting the floor. Perhaps he had dropped a cup or one of the fireplace tools. He would have been watching from a window. The man looked at the house, animatedly, and then back at Doug. "I guess you could say it's been a little strange," he said. "No one to talk to. But sometimes I prefer it that way."

Doug said nothing. The man flashed a half-grin, accompanied by a certain hardening of the eye. Doug did not care for it. He stood, ready to move quickly if needed, well aware of the stakes. His hatchet was lashed to the outside of his backpack and its blade cover could be removed in two swift motions. Unbutton and pull. His folded knife was in his pocket.

"Why don't we continue this conversation inside by the fire?" the man said. "It's cold out here. Your boy can tell me what it's like living all alone in the mountains with his daddy." The last word felt like a taunt.

"We'll talk here."

The man looked almost as if he had hoped this was what he would say. "Aren't you going to invite me in?" He was practically mocking Doug.

"No."

The man considered. He declared in his over-friendly tone, "Well, I'd call that inhospitable." It was almost as though he were speaking to himself. "Not sure it's really your roof and your fire to be denying shelter to travelers."

"You're not coming in." Doug could feel his heart beating. His tongue was thick in his mouth, but the words came out clearly.

"You don't own that hut."

"What are your intentions."

"My intentions?"

"I said what do you want?"

"I want to sit by your fire."

"And after that?"

"I need a place to sleep tonight."

"You hiking out of these mountains?"

"I haven't decided."

"Haven't decided?"

"Want to see who's around first. What others."

"And then?"

"And then decide."

"You can't sleep here."

"Not enough beds?"

"You get on back."

"Back where?"

"Partner, you get the fuck back to where you came from, and you do it now or I will put you down."

They faced each other. He felt a rage inside him. This ridiculous wordplay here on a ridgeline straddling life and death. The man would not touch the boy. He had never been so certain of anything. Nothing else mattered. He would tear the man's throat out with his teeth if he had to. He reached into his pocket and fingered the knife. Hefted its weight. Even in his terror he longed to wield it and put an end to this charade. Soon it would be time. He had thought only to strike in defense and as a last resort, but he realized he would have to attack instead. And he must commit to the issue. Like a lion clamping down and holding fast, no matter how the hooves fly. There could be no half-measures in this place with nothing between his child and this man but his own two hands. The hands God gave him. He nerved himself. He would wait until the man began speaking his retort and move then. When he was not braced for it. He would use everything he had. The knife. It was time. But the threat, and the momentum behind it, did the work for him. The man's affect changed like a tire punctured. His shoulders slumped as he asked in a whining tone, "But what am I supposed to eat? I don't have any food to get myself back to the observatory. It took me seven hours to hike here."

Doug took care not to betray his relief. In his other pocket was an energy bar. He tossed it to the man, who caught it, surprised. He looked down at it and studied the wrapper. Doug knew there was plenty of food at the observatory, rooms full of it. Far more than they had. Food enough to feed a rugby team. And he had ample daylight left to make the return hike, especially if he could retrace the freshly broken trail. Whether he made the trip in comfort or even safety was not Doug's concern. An immigrant who lands on an international flight and cannot clear passport control must turn around and fly back home. She is exhausted and demoralized and does not want to make the return flight. But she can do it. If she must.

The man muttered in poor humor. "Real friendly neighbors.

Ask to warm up by the fire and get threatened for it. Don't come around the observatory asking me for any favors."

"Don't come back here. You've been warned."

"Why would I want to come back here? You seem like awful company to me." He looked at the energy bar again as though he could not believe the turn of events. "You're really going to send me away with this and that's it?"

"You won't starve. Now go."

He turned and began to walk with his uneven gait toward Mount Adams and the observatory beyond it. His backpack looked half full and packed without care, the light items on the bottom and the heavy, bulky ones on top. Doug watched him walk for quite some time. He did not stop or turn around, and he made steady progress. Eventually Doug released the knife handle, which had imprinted into his palm the lines and screws of craftsmen or hunters, or both.

* * *

Tim realized that something serious had occurred but did not quite understand what it was. It was unclear how much he had overheard beyond the man's wild laugh. He had been inside, and the windows and door had been closed. The two men had not raised their voices or shouted. He asked few questions beyond what the man had wanted and seemed to sense that his father was not in a mood to be interrogated. He did gather that their new life had been threatened in some fundamental way. When Doug returned inside, he gave his son his best reassuring smile. It was not convincing. He had risen to the moment but to do so had shocked his system. When the adrenaline dissolved away, he found himself feeling ill and noticed that his hands were shaking. As a fundamental matter, he did not believe in violence and had never borne such an encounter before. He made an excuse of putting the wood they had gathered for their desk project in the dormitory to give himself something to do. There he had something resembling a mild panic attack.

The man's sheepish retreat had altered nothing. He had switched demeanors like changing coats, as the weather required. The look on his face and the note of ugly patronizing humor in his voice had been real, whatever had followed. He had sounded out his neighbor as a traveler tests the thinness of ice. He was prepared to take what he could. Doug believed this. Whether that meant their food, their rifle, their solitude, a seat at their table, or something more sinister was hard to say. He probably did not know his own intentions and was improvising to see how far to go. It was possible that he was nothing worse than unpleasant company: an unctuous priest or an unnerving tenant. He was unwell, that much was clear. It had been right to deal with him harshly. Hadn't it? Had invoking violence been an overreaction? The man had not made any actual threat. Doug never would have behaved aggressively before coming to this place. He had always been quick to resolve conflicts with a smile or a joke, a word at his own expense. Yet today he had behaved like an animal. He tried to reassure himself about the man he had chased away. His actions and movements had been unpredictable. And if he had been frightened off, it was only through the threat of force. He was like a person you would cross the street to avoid. A homeless man raising his voice for no good reason, or someone aggressively talking to himself. Doug did not want him around—did not want his company and did not want him near his son. He was not welcome.

The experience changed everything about the way they would have to live, he realized. They would need to secure the hut. Thankfully its doors and windows had locks. They were not strong enough to keep out a determined intruder, but at least no one could sneak in some night while they were asleep. They must begin locking up as a matter of course. The snow was another point of defense. As soon as the next big snowfall covered the man's tracks, they would be able to see if anyone had approached or drawn near. This was not something they had seen any reason to do before. They always left the hut in the other direction, to the north, to gather wood and water. But at midday, when the sun shone brightly over the area leading south to Mount Washington, he could glass the ridgeline with binoculars and spot any fresh prints. Contingency planning would also need to come into play. During the encounter, he had told himself that there was no room to fail. He thought: the boy has no way to retreat and nowhere to go if something happens to me. He would be left in the hands of this unstable person who might mean him harm. Plainly that was insufficient. The disordered thoughts of a panicked moment. There must be a plan B. Where should the boy go if matters became desperate? To another hut in the Presidential Traverse? To the world below? The best solution, Doug decided, was down Mount Madison and to the ranger station a mile from their parking lot. It might be empty, but it stood the best chance of any nearby structure of being inhabited. There would be shelter and eventually communications. It would be a long journey, but the boy could make it if he had to. They would need to rehearse how to get there using maps, even if they could not reach it on the snowbound trails.

The most important point of defense was the rifle. It could no longer lie collecting dust on a high shelf in the great room. Doug needed to get it out, make sure it was operable, and learn how to use it. He had only fired a gun once before in his life, at a pistol range with a friend in Connecticut. That had been five years earlier. He was no marksman, although he could hit a large target inside of thirty feet with some reliability. But he needed to become familiar with loading the rifle quickly, operating its safety catch, and discovering any quirks in its sighting or action so that they would not surprise him in a moment of decision. He would also have to teach the boy to shoot. Both their lives could depend on it. He wondered whether the sound of rifle shot would carry all the way to the observatory. Surely not. But if so, it could serve as a useful deterrent to their visitor and frighten him out of any thought of a return. Then again, the sound could be heard by anyone. Who knew if someone below might hear it and become curious to know who was taking target practice high in the mountains. Their sanctuary was precarious. One unstable hiker had unbalanced it. If someone or some group more competent or determined arrived and decided to take what was theirs, Doug would be unable to stop them. Militias could be roaming the countryside below. Or perhaps such thoughts were as unhinged as their visitor. There was no way to know. He decided he would muzzle the barrel instead of attracting unnecessary attention.

These preparations were not geared solely toward their neighbor, but he was Doug's chief concern. He might not come back. Doug had succeeded in frightening him away. But they could not rely on that sort of wishful thinking. The man could return. Doug had humiliated him. He could decide to take the hut for himself. Or its supplies. Or his revenge. They must be ready. His son watched his father in awe as he weighed these awesome considerations by the fire. He had never displayed violence before the boy and did not hold up chest-thumping as any sort of virtue. Yet his son had just watched him threaten to take apart an intruder, like some raw frontiersman. Whatever the boy had heard, it was clear that the gist of the exchange was not lost on him. There was nothing for it. He had to survive and protect his son in this harsh new landscape.

There arose the question of how much to try to explain. The child must likewise take the threat seriously. Doug could play it off as nothing and let Tim forget about it. Why make him worry about something over which he had no control? Why not give him a lighthearted childhood as best he could— to replicate the experience he would have in his home. No. What had occurred that afternoon was a matter of urgency. They must be on their guard. The boy needed to look out for their only neighbor, whom they must assume to be hostile. They had been careless. This was no mountaintop getaway or seasonal retreat. It was a hideout while the rest of the world came unglued. Their visitor had been a warning and a reminder of other threats abroad. Whatever danger he posed going forward, he was not their only problem. Their safety must become every bit as pressing as buckling a seat belt or looking both ways before crossing a street. Doug would need to find the right words and make the boy wary without terrifying him.

He would work the thought into conversation in the coming days. And let the boy see him locking doors and working on the rifle. For now, he said:

"If you see that man, I want you to let me know right away. OK?"

"OK."

"No keeping it to yourself. He's the kind of person who would hold up a finger to his lips and try to have a secret with you. If you saw him nosing around here."

"I'll tell, I promise."

"I don't think he'll come back. He's staying at the observatory on Mount Washington. There's plenty of space and food for him there."

"Why did he come here then?"

"I think he was looking to see who else is around."

"Did he want to stay here?"

"I'm not sure what he wanted. I don't think he knew either. But I told him that he couldn't stay here with us."

Tim thought for a moment. "That's good. I like it better just us."

"Me too."

They watched the fire.

"Dad?"

"Yeah, sport?"

"Do you think he'll come back?"

"No. I told him not to."

"That wasn't very friendly."

"I know. I like being friendly. And I like you to be friendly. But every now and then you can't be as friendly with everyone. Because sometimes other people aren't friendly."

"Yeah." Tim thought. "Dad? Were you scared when he was here?"

"You know, I was scared. I didn't like the look of him. I wasn't sure what he would do. I didn't want him around here."

"I was scared too."

"Were you?"

"Yeah. I was worried something might happen to you."

"Nothing's going to happen to me, my guy. And he's gone now."

"And you told him not to come back."

"That's right. And I don't think he will. Let's make dinner."

"Can we still have breakfast for dinner?"

"We can still have breakfast for dinner. Pancakes or egg whites?"

"Definitely pancakes."

"Alright. That's what I thought you'd say. Let's put our aprons on."

✳✳✳

Snow and snow again. Thanksgiving came and went. Winter approached their cabin with a sharper bite to the air and a gray permanence to the sky. It was no longer possible to be outside for any length of time without full cold-weather gear, and the afternoons of comfortable sunshine came to an end. The wind would pick up and carry for hours, rather than minutes, at a stretch, whistling in the windows and making them thankful for their shelter. When they left its comforts, the icy air stabbed at their uncovered wrists and necks. Doug stopped shaving altogether to avoid its slap on his face. His beard grew whiter than the last time he had worn one, when

Tim was a baby. It was not the only sign of age on his person. The change from a sedentary life to an active one as a homesteader and a child's playmate had strengthened him but also created new aches. His limbs were strong, but his back was never completely free of pain. Petty ailments that used to come and go during his days in the city now lingered as he demanded more from his body. He felt the incipient grinding of arthritis deep in the throat-clearing reaches of his spine. When he stood up, he took a few moments to straighten out completely, like a bent stem rebounding from the weight of overnight frost. He had taken care to look after their dental health to avoid any high-altitude crises, but his teeth were yellower than he liked. He imagined them enduring alongside his creaking and time-whitened bones. His face showed more lines around the eyes and cheeks as he dropped weight and clung to lean muscle. He tightened his belt one and then two notches. There was a certain empty space above his eyelids and beneath his jawline, as the ordeal wore away lymph and fatty tissue to reveal the bare essence of his hollow face in middle age. His hands seemed larger against his angular wrists and forearms, and they dangled low beyond his waist as time both strengthened and sagged the vessel for his waking spirit.

The boy changed as well. He was undergoing a growth spurt. His baby fat seemed to disappear, and he lengthened almost daily, to the point where his ankles showed at the bottom of one of his three pairs of pants. The structure of his adult face had begun to come into relief, and it was possible to imagine what he would look like as a man. Large blue eyes. Smooth round cheeks sprinkled with freckles that would hopefully stay. A button nose. Quizzical eyebrows. A good chin. A mouth made for singing and laughter. His new, leaner proportions sometimes caused his father to do a double-take and confirm that the person walking by was in fact the child he had known from birth. How could he keep growing? What height would he eventually reach? Doug had always thought he would like it best when his son gained adulthood and they could converse together as friends and equals. But now he saw that this had been an impatient and foolish projection. Each age for the boy was the right age. And while, looking back, he had his favorite seasons of the child's life to date, he would not exchange any one for another. He was ready for each when it came, and he missed it when it was gone. But by then it was time for the next. Perhaps the next had already arrived. He would only know in retrospect.

The desk project gained momentum as they completed the outdoor portion of the work in the first week of December. The tasks took Doug's mind off other things. He thought of David, and the choices he had made during the storm. Often, he wondered whether it had been a mistake to let the weather force them to stay in the mountains for the winter. As he rose each day, he came to dread the steady failure that greeted him on each communications check. He also began to worry about their dwindling supply of food. He was stretching their pantry with a rotation, but the boy had begun to complain and leave a half-finished plate when less-favored items were served. It was important to complete the outdoor gathering now, before even heavier snow made the trip to and from the timberfall more arduous and eventually buried their worksite. They had already had difficulty finding it once after a two-day storm, but Doug had insisted they go so as not to let it be covered completely.

Once they had what they needed, they could move the work inside. At the small workbench they had established in the cold end of the great room, they could focus on cutting and shaping, sanding and joining. The work required patience and helped to teach the boy to persevere. Their first and most promising disk for the desktop split while Doug sanded it, showing that he had cut too thin a cross section. They had other cross sections of a similar width that they set aside and would use in double only as a last resort. It took a week to harvest and haul six potential desktops and five potential stool tops of nearly uniform width and quality. Such was the shape of the tree from which they took the desktops that the cross sections bore a pleasing asymmetrical shape not unlike the nation of France. By the last trip to the timberfall, they were suffering through the sawing, with Tim impatient and Doug letting the cold affect the precision of his cut. He decided they had enough lumber to end their collecting. Between the flats and the two dozen–odd branches for legs, there was ample room for error in the coldest months ahead. They packed up the saw and with relief stopped making their daily trips into the forest for wood.

As they dragged the last pieces onto the hut's deck at dusk, Tim looked up and exclaimed. "Dad! A comet!"

They both turned their gazes skyward and watched a silent blaze trace an arc between two clouds. It seemed impossibly close. There was no fear of being struck, but the object was flying directly over the national forest.

"Quick, Timmy, grab those binoculars."

Tim picked up a pair from the deck and studied the object as it passed. "It doesn't look like a comet. It's shiny." He passed the binoculars to his father, who raised them just in time to see.

"You're right. That's metal reflecting. And it's on fire. It almost looks like . . ." He lowered the binoculars.

"Almost looks like what?"

"Like a satellite."

"But why is it falling?"

Doug tried to glass the object once more, but it had disappeared from view. "Come on. Let's get inside."

***

They fell into a new domestic rhythm with fewer trips out of doors. Some days they hardly went outside, except to the privy to empty the chamber pot. They continued to urinate in the outhouses in daylight, but sitting on the freezing commode was almost intolerable, especially after it began to frost over. And Doug allowed them to become lazy and use the chamber pot for the first and last call of nature each day, when it was cold and dark and neither of them wanted to put on boots and coats. He continued to split wood for the fire and cleaned the solar panel and its connection points daily. These activities kept his boots and jacket in use. They rarely used David's room because it was so cold there. They ran the space heater long enough each day to keep the telecommunications equipment from freezing and to make the daily check for news from the outside world. News never came. Some days, the weather was so overcast with so little sunlight that they could not generate a sufficient charge to operate the computer or space heater. They also exchanged books in David's small library. Gibbon was very slow going as Doug proceeded through the Antonines. The main lesson he drew from Roman history was a warning against the failure to

transfer power peacefully. Each outgoing emperor seemed to surrender the office only by being murdered. Murdered by troops,
and therein lay the second lesson: to keep the military out of
politics. After the first volume of Gibbon, he took a break and
switched to *Middlemarch*, another long and tedious read that
nevertheless rewarded his persistence. Its large cast of characters and their petty provincial squabbles made for friendly, small
stakes at such a dire historical moment. He also found that he
enjoyed reading a book that depicted the passage of time at a
point in his life when his own days crawled by interminably.

Their new life began to replace the old. The biggest change
aside from isolation was living in a world with nothing to anticipate. Doug realized how much of his daily existence had
involved drifting toward little life preservers. A package expected
in the mail. A new movie premiering over the weekend. Dinner
from a favorite takeout spot. He'd had no idea how much he
passed the rungs of life's ladder hand over hand through daily
monotony to keep him going. Here there was nothing to look
forward to—or, at least, nothing so tangible. There was no question of acquiring some new physical object to deliver a jolt of
endorphins. Or still less of obtaining that jolt through the act of
making a purchase, hearing a concert, or meeting a friend. Instead, he must take comfort in less ephemeral pleasures. Rising
with the sun. His good health. The morning coffee. Writing in
his journal. Taking exercise: the push-ups and pull-ups he performed ritualistically before breakfast, or his yoga-like stretching.
Spending time with his boy. He knew that he would look back
and be glad of these sacred months they had together. More
than that, it might well turn out to be the best season of his
life. Yet knowing this as an abstract matter and willing himself

to appreciate it while it dripped by in confusion and tedium were two distinct things. It was the difference between a bag of potato chips and a bowl full of kale. The kale was unquestionably better nourishment. Any fool knew it. He simply had not yet grown used to eating nothing but bitter leafy greens. He would have liked to be able to sneak the occasional salty chip.

They had been in the hut by themselves for so long that life from before began fading away. It was not that he forgot riding on a subway car or sleeping in linen sheets, walking the city or laughing with other adults. Those things had simply receded from his active thoughts. Rather than missing them suddenly, as he had done in the fall, he had to summon them to his consciousness, at which point they appeared like half-remembered abstractions. *Right*, he would think. *I did that. I guess I miss that. But not as much as I would have thought.* And then he interrogated the thought. Was that right? Did he miss it? He missed the feelings, but he did not necessarily miss the experiences that had delivered them. Yet this was not the same as deciding he did not want to enjoy those experiences once more. If they would again become possible. He felt no need to return to an office or endure a commute. But he remembered leaving his office for an hour on a crisp fall afternoon to walk the city streets. That was a bargain he would strike again. Perhaps he was in some sort of post-traumatic state of shock. For a creature of habit, he surprised himself by being more adaptable than he would ever have guessed. The new life here in the mountains was suiting him, he thought, even as a sort of low-level depression burned like a candle in an empty room. All the same, he knew that when he was able to leave this place, there would be things *here* that he would miss—and aspects to his previous life he would just as soon not revisit. Here, at least, he was not pitied as a widower, badgered to date again but unable to use friendships to fill the void that Carol had left behind. Here he had Tim: he was redefining his existence in relation to his child. Being a parent had become his primary identity.

At first, the thought of surviving the winter was so pressing that he did not allow himself to think of spring. Would they stay or leave? How would they know when it was safe to descend the mountain? By spring the disruption might have ended. It could be safe to retreat from their redoubt. There might be no need to stay hidden away, and instead they could rejoin the world and resume their lives. Yet he knew there was a good chance that they would remain in the dark about the state of the world when the seasons changed. And then they would need to decide what to do. They could hike out and take their chances. Or they could stay burrowed in, well away from danger, until safety beckoned to them unmistakably. The Second World War had lasted six years. The Civil War had lasted four. It seemed unrealistic to assume that this conflict, whatever it was, would be over in a few short months. Trying to gauge its duration with a few snippets of outdated information was an exercise in self-delusion. He had initially thought it would flame out in days, then weeks, and then he had realized with a sinking feeling that it was an indefinite crisis. He suspected it would likely be measured not in months but in years. But his need for optimism would not allow him to concede such a devastating forecast. So he tried to avoid the topic with himself. Yet he couldn't, quite. He thought even before the crisis ended, perhaps the period of frightening instability would conclude in spring and it would be safe to descend. Civilization might be restored; border crossings might once more be possible. They could go home in something like normalcy without having to hide by themselves in an eagle's nest. There was no way to know.

It became difficult to keep up his spirits. As much as he enjoyed his son's company, Doug needed a break and some solitude. There was none to be had. He felt like a phone's battery permanently in the red, in need of a full and uninterrupted charging. Tim was a sweet boy, sensitive and self-sufficient in many ways. But any seven-year-old had needs that overwhelmed the resources of a full-time, all-the-time parent. He was all id, moving from one obsession to the next, fixated entirely on whatever was directly in front of him or at the top of his mind. Whether it was his spaceship toy or the desk project, baking the snickerdoodles or building a snowman, the boy—like any child of his age—knew only one gear, and he drove it at top speed. A child was by nature an extremist and had not lived enough life to learn how to slow down at turns. Doug wanted to mirror the boy's enthusiasms and keep up the morale of the hut by joining in whatever urgent game or task or goal consumed his every waking thought. But to do so constantly, without interruption, during a time of dread, uncertainty, and physical discomfort, at times became overwhelming. On those evenings, he drank.

Always he did so when the boy had gone to sleep, and never to excess. There was ample wine, and there was David's bottle of Scotch. He did not allow himself more than two full drinks any evening on the chance that some calamity or danger required his reflexes or judgment. None had since their unwelcome visitor. But sometimes he needed to forget the day. Its stresses or its numbing monotony. The pain in his back or his knee. Friends he may have lost but did not know about for sure. His unmet need for adult company. For female company. Sorrow about the state of the world below. Fears for the future. The boy's more than his, but—in his second glass—his as well. He did not want to spend the next half of his life as a refugee or a mountain hermit. There were places he wanted to see: Brazil, and Japan. He had never been to a desert or set foot in the Arctic tundra. He wanted to lay eyes on the Great Wall of China. Was any of that still possible?

His thoughts swirled, as unappealing as the final dregs in the bottle of red wine. He had finished his second glass, so he wouldn't pour out those dregs and drink them. Discipline remained important. Even when morale was low. Especially when morale is low, he told himself in the unsteady voice of a drinker trying to act sober. Enough. He had reached the end of another day. His son was safe. They were together. Tomorrow he would start fresh. He walked unsteadily to the kitchen, carefully washed his wine glass, and went to sleep.

***

When Tim sliced his hand with a saw, the blood was shockingly red against the snow. Pouring in a stream down his palm and off the tip of his thumb, it first dotted and then began to melt the powder. The contrast in colors of bright red against pure white gave a sickening lurch to the stomach, an instant creation of stakes. Here was the stuff of life where it should not be. There was only so much of it.

Doug's head snapped around as the boy squealed in pain and terror. It was the kind of scream every parent dreads hearing. Tim had been using the saw to even out potential stool legs to a uniform length. Doug had shown him how, and if he was not yet good at it, he was improving. It was important to the boy to have real tasks as they went about the desk project. He knew make-work when he saw it. Carrying things from here to there, or clearing an area of clutter, or drawing out evenly spaced hash marks on unseen surfaces that were never used— these didn't really contribute, and coming up with such tasks took more time than actually teaching the boy how to help. Doug had told himself that he would supervise the use of sharp or pointed tools and that his son was sensible. Children this age had been helping on farms for centuries.

He didn't supervise closely enough. And he didn't insist on gloves during the work. He had tried to require them but there were only the two adult pairs of leather gloves, and they were much too big. They made gripping the saw impossible. Tim would start with them on but remove first one and then the other as he proceeded. If his father told him to put them back on, they would descend into arguing. "Everyone has their own way of doing it, Dad," the boy said. "I saw best when I can actually *use my hands*." Insisting in the face of this obstinacy grew exhausting and could sour an entire afternoon. Yet safety around a sharp blade was the place to draw the line. He should have taken the tool away until the boy agreed to wear the gloves. Or at least made him wear his well-fitting cold-weather gloves for some level of protection. But he hadn't. The saw had slipped as Tim notched and re-notched it into his groove as he tried to work himself into a rhythm of cutting the wood. He pushed too hard, his left hand gripped the wood too close to the notch, and the blade came loose and sunk into his hand with the force of his frustration behind it. He was bleeding profusely before he knew what had happened.

The cut was deep but clean and made with a sharp instrument free of rust. It was on the meat of his hand between his thumb and his wrist. It didn't seem as though any tendons had been cut. Doug directed him to wiggle his fingers, and he was able to do so with facility but much pain. Blood flowed freely and stained the snow. He whimpered in panic, his eyes wide.

"Timmy, this is what we're going to do."

"It hurts!" His feet moved in a terrified dance.

"Timmy? *Timmy!*" The boy met his gaze. Tears spilled onto his cheeks. "I know it hurts, buddy. Be brave." The boy nodded, tears still streaming. "Look at me and listen to my voice. Here's what we're going to do. There are four steps. First thing is we'll stay calm. Second thing is we'll stop the bleeding. Third thing is we'll wash the cut and make sure it's clean. Fourth thing is we'll get it fixed and bandaged. Sound like a plan?"

"OK but can we hurry?"

"Let's hurry. Come on, we'll go inside and get that big first aid kit. It will have everything we need. We're already doing step one by staying calm."

He held his bandana on the child's cut and applied pressure as they entered the cabin. Warm blood soaked through and stained his hands, casting the whorls of his fingerprints into relief. Suddenly the boy said he felt sick, and the color drained from his face, leaving dark purple circles under his eyes. He appeared likely to faint. Doug sat him on the table and held the bandana on while his son leaned into him heavily. His head lolled on his thin neck as it had done when he was a baby and was too small to raise its awesome weight. Doug caressed the boy's hair with the other hand as he swooned, eager to get to the first aid kit but aware that, for the moment, reassurance of this kind was more important than tending to the injury. Sweat beaded on the child's forehead and matted his hair. He came around slowly and, after overcoming his confusion, began to cry softly into the breast of his father's jacket.

"I just want to go home," he said miserably. "When can we go home?" His strength and defenses had left him. This was how he felt in his moment of greatest weakness. Doug willed himself strength for what he must do.

He gave the boy one of his rarest and favorite treats while washing and examining the wound: the use of his smartphone to navigate and explore. He needed a powerful distraction while he set about his work. The boy nimbly flicked through apps, pictures, and old videos with his one free hand, occasionally wincing as his father cleaned and studied the injury. It continued to bleed whenever pressure was removed. The cut was an inch long and half an inch deep, which for his tiny frame meant halfway through his hand. Miraculously, the part of the saw that had cut him was not a serrated segment of blade, so the injury was perfectly straight rather than a jagged gash. After cleaning it with water and then alcohol, which stung and brought a rebuke, Doug taped gauze over it tightly and made a search of the large first aid kit they had brought from the Mount Washington observatory. The cut would need to be closed in order to heal; it was too deep to knit up on its own quickly enough to avoid infection. He desperately hoped to find skin glue of the type he had once received as treatment in lieu of stitches for a deep but straight cut on his forehead. But two tours of the bag revealed none, and he suspected that for a young child, skin glue on an active part of the body like a hand would not answer. The cut would need to be sewn.

A stitches bag was part of the first aid kid. Tim would never have believed this, but the sight of the needle in this context terrified his father as much as it frightened him. Doug unzipped the bag out of the boy's field of view and studied its contents. More gauze and tape. Butterfly bandages. Surgical gloves. Medical scissors. Three sealed syringe packets. A vial of lidocaine. Needles. Sterile thread. He scanned the accompanying pamphlet for lidocaine dosage amounts, which were based on patient weight. Tim weighed just fifty pounds. The rudimentary stitching instructions made the procedure sound comically easy. Clean wound and rub using isopropyl wipes. Numb wound area. Allow five to seven minutes for anesthetic to take effect. Pinch separated skin together. Sew using even, parallel stitches approximately three millimeters apart. Tie off thread tightly at end. Clean and disinfect again. Bandage tightly. Clean and change dressings daily as needed. Remove stitches after seven to ten days. Simple as a pie crust.

He wanted to steel himself with a drink but knew he needed his faculties. He did not have the steadiest hands, and his fingers trembled at the best of times. He explained to the boy what needed to be done.

"Do I have to have a shot?"

"Yes. I have to give you a shot."

Tim whimpered. He was terrified of needles. "I don't think I need one. If we just put a new Band-Aid on it each day, it will get better without a shot."

"No, buddy. The cut is too deep. You need stitches or it won't heal. It will get infected, and you could get very sick. And you can't have stitches without a shot. The point of the shot is so you won't feel any pain during the stitches. The shot is good because it makes your hand feel numb and your hand won't hurt anymore."

They discussed it back and forth for some time. Tim reasoned and pleaded but seemed to know he was only forestalling the inevitable. During the last phase of their negotiation, they held hands, and eventually they sat together quietly for a while. At last, it was time to begin the procedure. Doug had half a moment's thought of giving the child a drink to steady *his* nerves. At least one of them could have a taste of Scotch. Thankfully, the phone had been fully charged and could be browsed and played on for hours yet. He set up a divider of sorts using one of the hanging curtains like medical drapery so that Tim could not watch the work being done. He wanted to see the initial injection, but he should not view the stitching. After carefully measuring the dosage of anesthetic, tapping out bubbles, and triple-checking it against the weight chart, he told Tim the importance of holding still.

"Now, the shot will hurt. But it won't hurt nearly as bad as getting this cut did. I want you to be brave and not squirm. If you move, we might have to do the shot again. So do your best. Ready?"

The boy exhaled slowly and spoke to himself in a whisper. His father caught the words: "You can do it, Tim," he said to himself. "OK. Ready."

"Here we go. Tell me ten things you know about the Titanic. Starting *now*."

The boy began reciting dates and names in a high, fast voice. The unsinkable Molly Brown. The lifeboat count. The number of souls aboard and the number lost to the deep. How many staterooms and how many promenades, or decks, were contained in each. The strangest fact: only two bathtubs for the entirety of the steerage class. For a brief moment, Doug had the presence of mind to wonder if this could possibly be true. As the boy spoke, he watched the approaching needle with one eye, but at the last minute squeezed both eyes shut tightly and continued his strange nautical catechism. Pricking his skin with the needle was difficult to do. The needle slid in easily, but Doug found that willing himself to break the surface took effort and courage. He held some deep primitive conviction that the skin of his child was inviolable. But he administered the dose, in what he supposed would be called the distal portion of the meat under the boy's thumb, on the far side from his body with his palm facing up. As he recalled from dental injections of Novocain, he must be deliberate about delivering the medicine. It was not an inoculation. One practitioner had described the sensation to him as too much needle filling too small a space. This was the liquid saturating the tissue. The boy kept his eyes shut and said nothing. His father attempted to project confidence and experience, as though he had done this many times before. He spoke in quiet words of steady reassurance as though calming an animal. After he removed the needle, Tim exhaled and made sure there would be no more shots. When his father confirmed this, the boy became euphoric.

"Toughest part is over," Doug said.

"You know, it wasn't as bad as I thought it would be," Tim said.

"I'm proud of you."

For Tim, the ordeal was now done. For his father, it was about to begin. He used the numbing period to wash his hands once more and don surgical gloves. Then he bathed the wound in iodine, cleaned it, and rubbed it with isopropyl wipes. After satisfying himself that the area was thoroughly numb by pricking the surrounding skin with the syringe and getting no reflex or reaction, he prepared to begin. Tim by this time was focused on the phone and no longer as interested in the work on his hand. The drapery prevented him from watching the next part of the procedure. Using his backpacking headlamp to see clearly, Doug ensured that there was no debris or foreign particle in the wound area. Then he made his initial pass with the needle. His first stitch was clumsy and tentative but his second was better. The manual in the stitch kit gave a diagram of how to approach the task. He realized he was hunched over with his nose almost touching the boy's arm, and relaxed his posture, allowing the pain of tension to dissipate. He was so intent on the work that he had forgotten to blink, and his eyes felt salty and irritated. By the third stitch, he felt more confident in his needlepoint and began to wish he had practiced on something from the kitchen before sewing up his child. As he gauged the spacing, he decided that four stitches would serve. At one point, Tim forgot himself and began to reach his injured hand to his nose to scratch an itch. Doug's nerves were strained to the breaking point, but he avoided speaking sharply and instead allowed the blunder to break the tension. He continued his work. When it came time to finish, he first brought the two flaps of loose skin together, tightening the thread like a shoelace. He watched the boy for any sign of reaction. He feared that the anesthetic might soon wear off. While tying off the suture he cursed his lack of dexterity. He kept at it until he had brought the thread in upon itself tightly in a knot that was unlovely but seemed likely to hold. Cleaning the exterior of the cut once more with a sterile wipe, he prepared a bandage with a strong adhesive. Finally, he showed off his handiwork.

"See?" he said, removing the curtain and inviting the boy to look.

"Uggghh!" Tim said, disgusted and curious at once. The dark thread stood out against his pale skin, the tied-off ends protruding rigid and sharp like a black shuttlecock. Traces of blood still remained on his hand. "Gross!"

"Four stitches. Your first."

"Will it look like that forever?"

"No. We'll take the stitches out in a week or two. That's the black part. And the cut will get better. The stitches hold the skin together so it can heal. We'll change the bandage. But you'll probably have a little white scar there. Like this, see?" He showed the boy the scar on his wrist where he had put his hand through a windowpane during a game of tag at age eleven or twelve, requiring stitches of his own. His mother had panicked, knowing that people commit suicide by cutting themselves there. A hub of important veins and vessels. What if he bled to death before they got to the emergency room? The glass had been so thin, like the sacred skin.

"A scar would be cool. Something to remember our time in the mountains. I wish I could show Mom."

Doug looked at his son as the boy studied his hand. Such a bracing point of view. Often the uncanny satisfaction of parenting was recognizing himself, or Carol, in a look or mannerism of the child's. But moments like this presented an even deeper mystery. Here was a new perspective that was nevertheless the yield of his own issue. Doug would never have thought of the scar as a commemoration. And he had not yet allowed himself to think past their experience this year to a time of safe reflection. He knew that he had cauterized his emotions. There was no one to express them to. But the boy was right. Such a day would come. He should will himself to believe it just as his son unthinkingly assumed it. How had he acquired this wisdom? He was only a child. But he also possessed an effortless serenity as he interacted with the world. Partly this was his own unique nature. He was less worrisome than his parent. And, in part, it was bound up in his innocence. He assumed that the future would be safe because he did not know how dangerous the world really was. Maybe that innocence was his version of hope. And perhaps that was, at bottom, all they needed to survive. But hope was more elusive than innocence because it entailed choosing to believe despite knowing the reasons not to. Innocence was by its nature ephemeral. How to preserve it as long as he could? Maybe that wasn't the right question. How to come to terms with its inevitable loss? Doug had no notion of its value until he became a father and saw it firsthand. It sustained him. It was a miracle.

⁂

After the winter solstice, the days began to lengthen, even as the weather grew more fierce. Eighty days and more on their own. They had a simple Christmas, with a few treats from the storeroom that they had set aside for their dinner, and a crude toy race car that Doug had whittled in the evenings for a gift. He had also found a much-loved bag of green plastic toy soldiers and placed them in a hiking sock to serve as a Christmas stocking. They smelled faintly of petroleum and seemed to date to the Kennedy administration. Troops in webbed helmets held rifles ending in bayonets. Some prepared to toss grenades. Others braced in an infantry march. Heroes from wars of another time. Men with fathers of their own and sons they had never seen. Tim had drawn Doug a picture for a gift and presented it proudly. It was an ocean liner like the grand sailing palaces of the early twentieth century, which he had named the SS *Christmas*. Below it, in the boy's unique hand, read: "To: Dad. Mary Christmas. Love, Timmy." Before going to bed on Christmas Eve, they doused the fire so that Santa Claus could enter the hut without scorching his boots. First, they warmed stones in the fireplace and used them to heat their beds. On the boy's insistence, they also made a batch of cookies and set two out on the mantle with a glass of condensed milk. They ate the others.

On Christmas morning, the child woke with the same excitement he showed every year. The day, to him, remained a source of magic. His father had difficulty sleeping, worrying that Tim would be disappointed when his secret hope of a roomful of shining presents did not materialize. But he showed great resilience and maturity. He had been so deprived of new toys that the meager wooden car and army green soldiers were novel and fresh. He instantly set about devising battle scenarios around the room and making gunnery noises and explosions. Snow fell softly outside, and Doug made a fire to warm the freezing space. He played Vince Guaraldi's forlorn Christmas album through his phone's small, tinny speaker. After finishing their late breakfast, still lingering in the pajamas, Tim declared himself satisfied.

"It wasn't the Christmas with the most presents," he said. "But it was a special Christmas."

"I thought so too."

"And it's not like we could just go shopping and buy stuff for each other this year."

"I wish we could have, buddy."

"Yeah. But I really liked my presents."

"And I love my drawing. The SS *Christmas*. Was that a real ship, or did you make it up for the holiday?"

The boy smiled winningly. "Guess you'll have to look it up!"

They sat together and watched the snow fall.

"Dad?"

"Yeah, pal?"

"Can we watch the movie on your phone of me and Mom hanging the ornaments?"

"I love that movie."

"Me too."

He pulled it up and they huddled together before the small screen. For some reason, they had been trimming the tree at dusk: close to Tim's bedtime. It would have been his third Christmas. Her last.

She was so lovely. Her hair was cut short, and it showed her graceful long neck. She spoke to Tim quietly as he removed ornaments from a box and handed them to her one at a time. She explained each in turn before hanging it. This one was Gran's. This one was Dad's, from when he was your age. Look, this one has your birthday on it. This one is a cello. Can you say cello? Their son repeated the last word of each sentence in his innocent lisp. He wore corduroy pants and shoes no bigger than seashells. Between them, in the blue twilight, the task became sacred. He had not yet received his first haircut. The reddish curls that fell about his ears were spun of a fine thread. As if the hand that made them wore white gloves and sang in a whisper. His wife spoke to the boy tenderly. Here was her happiest moment. He remembered the wool dress that she wore. It had always been his favorite. She wore it beautifully. And she had on her leggings and her slippers. There was probably a mug of tea at hand. She had loved nothing better than to be enveloped in warmth.

"I really like the next part," Tim said next to him.

They watched as his younger self reached down to pick up a piece of tinsel and his mother stole a kiss on the nape of his neck. As she did so she breathed him in deeply. The child hardly seemed to notice and kept working. On the phone's small screen, she watched him with a little smile. Her face bore an expression of radiance. In the cabin, Tim looked up and saw that his father was weeping. Tears flowed down his cheeks like water. He looked at his son and smiled as best as he could. As the video continued to play, he wept for all he had lost. The love of his life. His life itself, just after he had started to put it back together. His understanding of the world. Any hope for the future. Tim had not seen this before and confusion passed over his face. But then, with his mother's ease, he resolved his doubts by putting his arms around his father's neck and hugging him close, and patting him on the back, as he had seen others do.

SIX

Two months passed. Snow-ins and fires. Fierce storms. Cabin fever. Gradually lengthening days but very little sun. Sweater upon sweater, and fingerless wool gloves indoors. Endless board games. The completion of old books and the starting of new ones. *The Chronicles of Narnia* for the two of them. *Anna Karenina* for Doug. Monotony in their food. Monotony in their routine. A desire for an excursion of some kind, but no ability to leave and hike anywhere in the snow-socked mountains. Tim's first do-it-yourself haircut, which he squirmed and fidgeted his way through, complaining all the while about the itchiness along his neck. Doug's beard growing into its own, making him a proper man of the forest. Doug found he had a desire for a road trip, of all things. He wanted the simple ability to leave this place and go—to drive the open road, play music with the windows down, stop for a meal, stay overnight in a small hotel. To find a diner in some town square and dip fresh fries into a milkshake's whipped cream.

"One more game?" Doug asked from across the table. They had already played three in a row, and it was not yet noon.

Tim yawned. "Sure. Not like there's anything else to do."

They traded pieces from white to black for variety. Tim intentionally misplaced his queen-side bishop and knight to see if his father noticed. A wan smile. A familiar opening. Both castled. They played with half-lidded eyes. Outside, the snow fell like grains of sand filling an hourglass.

Rook.

Pawn.

Knight.

Pawn.

Queen.

Pawn.

On the game went. Where they had once slapped pieces onto squares, now they slid each one into place.

"Down to pawns and queens again," Doug said.

"I hate when games end this way. It's so boring."

"Call it?"

"No, let's play it out."

Doug's king led Tim's queen on a fruitless chase around the corner of the board. He lacked the energy to spring into offense and enliven the match. Tim eventually pushed over his king, resigning.

"Think I'll go read for a while."

"Sure, pal. I might write in my journal. Good game."

"Good game."

The highlight of their day.

***

Last night I dreamt of my mother. I dearly hope that she is safe. So much of my confidence comes from her, from having someone believe in me utterly. We once sat at a Red Sox game, and after someone hit a home run, she nudged me with her elbow and said, "You could do that." She was completely serious. Such a ridiculous yet soul-filling conviction. I took it for granted until I went off to college and realized how rare it is, to have an unequivocal fan. Not just for myself, but for anyone. Do I make Tim feel this way? I hope that I do. Thanking another person for their certainty in your own goodness seems impossible. By the time I was a parent myself and could appreciate it, too much time had passed for her to remember. Bullshit. She has never stopped thinking this way or forgotten a thing about her children. And she probably still believes I could hit a home run in Fenway Park. I will thank her properly the next time I see her. If I see her again.

❊❊❊

The boy was more and more helpful around the cabin. It was mainly from boredom that he agreed to chip in and contribute. His chores included making his bed, helping with kitchen prep and cleanup, sweeping out sawdust from their workstation, and general tidying such as dishwashing and dusting. There was no particular reason for them to reach a broom under the recesses of the dormitory beds to gather dust bunnies except to have something to do and to preserve a general sense of order and cleanliness. Thankfully, the hut had a store of hotel-level cleaning supplies to keep the facilities neat for guests—especially the high-spending full-board weekenders that David had described. Doug spared the boy any tasks associated with the chamber pot or outhouse. His hand had healed fully, although the scar would remain. They had long since come to rely on their store of lumber rather than going out to gather fresh wood. Doug told himself they would resupply in spring: the season that would never arrive but which he dreaded all the same. Spring meant decisions. They went together to get water. It was the coldest and most difficult task in the dead of winter. Keeping one's hands dry was critical, and most of the stream was frozen over. For much of February, they had to smash through the ice with a pike they kept nearby for that purpose. They carried pails of water back to their cabin and heated it for weekly baths.

They had finished the desk and stool after several stops and starts. Both of them approved of the finished project. It had a unique look but a strong, functional aspect. For lack of any ability to lacquer or varnish the furniture, they had gone overboard in their sanding. It was one of the tasks the boy could perform freely, now that he was gun-shy around sharp tools. He dedicated himself to finding and eliminating any bump or blemish. As a result, the desktop and the stool were undoubtedly smooth. Some twenty percent of the desk lay in a fine mist of sawdust on the floor. Doug's own obsession had been perfecting the evenness of the legs of the stool and desk, so that there was no play and they stood still and even when placed on the ground. Ideally, he would have affixed foam or rubber furniture tips under each, but none of these were at hand. Instead, he stood the stool or desk on the floor, checked for a wobble, flipped it over, sanded one or more legs, and repeated the process. Once it was complete, Tim quickly made the workstation his own, coloring superhero decorations and placing them about the area. He declared it off-limits to grown-ups. Performing his schoolwork became less of a challenge as he embraced a new self-sufficiency. He wanted to receive the work and complete it independently, checking in only for questions or troubleshooting. If his father looked over his shoulder or talked too much, he would physically shoo the adult away. As his eighth birthday approached, he saw himself reaching a milestone with implications for maturity. It was a good trend after so many months of relying on his parent to the point of occasionally clinging. Doug was happy to give him his space and use the time to catch up on his own reading or various tasks.

Their supplies had held up well with the exception of food, which continued to dwindle. Doug worried about their diminishing reserve and fretted over what to do. His disciplined rationing began to give way around the first of March, as he rotated past meals the boy simply would not eat. Canned tuna. Buckwheat biscuits instead of flour. Canned chowders that the boy tasted once and then had to fight back heaving up. Their favorites were long since gone. The granola bars and dry cereals Tim had lived on back home had been consumed and were now bitterly missed. No more canned fruit. No snickerdoodles since the new year. Coffee long gone. These were luxuries, but their absence made both man and boy peevish. Doug's thoughts turned once more to hunting. He had the rifle and had spotted game tracks several times near the timberfall. He had seen multiple deer. But he continued to fear drawing attention by firing. Who knew how far the sound of a rifle shot would carry at this altitude. It had not seemed worth the risk, back when they had stores in reserve.

There was food at the Mount Washington observatory. He distinctly recalled seeing rows and rows of every type of canned good and staple when he and Tim had toured the building. Re-filling the duffel bag would serve their needs and it would not be too heavy to transport. It would take ten minutes to choose the items he needed. Two obstacles stood in the way. The first was making the journey to and from the summit, through snow, in late winter conditions. Without the benefit of a fore-cast. The second was the possibility of encountering others, including the man in the orange socks. It had been over three months since his visit to their campus. They had seen no sign of him since. There was no way to know if he had returned to the observatory after that day or had left the national forest al-together. He had spoken like a man digging in for a long stay. If he was there, perhaps he could be avoided. The pantry and refrigerated storage were on a lower floor from the observato-ry's main cafeteria. It might be possible to slip in, take what he needed, and slip out undetected. Others could be there. Not just unstable people but dangerous ones bent on violence. And then there was the boy. Surely he could not bring his son with him on such a dangerous journey. But leaving him behind created its own type of peril. He could be stranded all alone. Doug could become lost or injured on the hike. He could en-counter persons unknown in the observatory or elsewhere on the trail. Something could delay him, causing the boy to panic and attempt a hasty search. If he did not return at all, he was unsure whether an eight-year-old could survive by himself in the mountains. Or for how long.

Yet if they did not replenish their food supply, their life in the hut would be possible for only a few weeks longer. He suspected they would give it up for reasons other than the con-sidered decision to descend. Perhaps he might find food at another of the mountain huts in the Presidential Traverse. There were a half dozen of them. Mount Washington had food, that much was known, but it was the most likely to be occupied. Then again, it was also the closest. He would have to increase his mileage to reach another hut. Most of the others would require passing right by Washington. Whatever safety this would gain would be offset by additional time and exposure in winter conditions high in the New Hampshire mountains. And whoever else might be watching.

He tried to push the problem away like an aching tooth or a concern over money. From his earlier life. Such things felt quaint now. He did not even know if money existed anymore.

***

"Why have you started carrying the gun when we go out?"

"Bears."

"Bears?"

"What do bears do in the winter?"

"They hibernate."

"Which means?"

Tim put on his professorial voice and began to recite facts that he knew well. "The sow finds a shelter for herself and her young, they eat as much as they can to store fat for the winter, and then they sleep through the coldest months of the year."

"*Very* good. And when winter ends?"

"They wake up?"

"They wake up. And if you had been sleeping for three or four months, what would you do first thing?"

"Poop!" The boy began to laugh hysterically and then

danced around jutting his bottom out and making gassy noises. His father watched him and smiled.

"Right. And after that, you'd want to eat. That's what bears do. When they're done hibernating, they are *hungry*."

"So are the bears around here done hibernating?"

"I don't know. I think probably not quite yet. It's still winter. There aren't any berries for them to eat yet. But winter will be over soon. That's why I've been bringing the rifle. As the snow melts and the ice disappears on the river, the bears will wake up and come out. And so it makes sense to have the rifle just in case."

"You would shoot a bear?"

"If it's her or us, I would. But I think a gunshot might also frighten a bear away. That would be much better."

"Where would you point the gun when you shot it?"

"Straight up into the air."

"And that would scare the bear away?"

"I think so."

They had resumed their afternoon walks, sloshing a narrow path around the hut campus. The snow still lay too deep to travel any distance, but temperatures on some afternoons crept above freezing, and the occasional bluebird day beckoned them outside. The top layer of snow would melt and then refreeze overnight, forming a hard crust through which their boots broke. The stream where they gathered water was nearly half unfrozen, and the tinkle of its music held the incipient sound of spring. Just as these developments promised to take hold and reveal the new season, a fresh snowfall would arrive, blanketing all once more. When walks were possible, Doug wore the binoculars as well as the rifle. They had not yet been able in the new year to reach one of the nearby summits to glimpse Mount Washington, but on clear days they could see for miles to the north and west. The world looked much as it had before. Sometimes, as he glassed the valley, he wondered if he had dreamt up the surge. They had been so isolated here, and there had been no indications from the world below for months. Yet that in itself was his proof. No Wi-Fi or cellular signal despite religious daily checks. No visitors. No one on an ATV and no ski party coming through for a night's shelter. And he remembered seeing the news stories with his own eyes. As well as the satellite. It was real. He knew it was real. Willing himself from the abstract to the concrete, he kept his eyes out for tracks or other signs of wildlife but saw only the small footprints and scat of rabbits and marmots. In the vast expanse of white, it was hard to tell where land became sky, or what separated thought from vision.

One day in mid-March, as they hiked beneath the timberline, he saw a doe. It was fifty yards away. They were downwind, and it had not yet spotted them.

"Look, Tim! A deer," he whispered. They froze.

"Oooh! I like its spots. Wait, what are you doing?"

Doug was unshouldering his rifle. He slowly kneeled and sighted the doe.

"We need to eat, buddy."

"You're going to shoot the deer?"

"Shhh! We're running out of food. We need to eat. That deer will feed us for weeks."

"You can't shoot the deer!"

He lowered the rifle and looked at the boy. "Tim, we're going to have to survive this way. We've eaten through most of the food in our hut. Soon we'll get hungry."

"Dad!"

He disregarded these urgent whispers and centered the deer into his sights as it looked up, ears wide. Wind blew across the plateau, swishing the low branches. He began to measure his breathing. Accuracy was important. He did not want a glancing shot.

"I'm not eating it."

"What? Tim, I've got to concentrate."

"If you kill it and bring it home, I'm not eating it. I'll eat anything else, I promise. Even clam chowder."

"I don't have time to argue."

His finger rested on the trigger. The deer watched them and stood completely still.

"Dad."

He looked at the boy, whose cheeks were now covered with tears. He was desperate on behalf of the animal. His eyes pleaded. Doug realized that the crisis was no longer about food but the space between him and his son. If he pressed ahead, he would violate it. Food or no food. He lowered the rifle.

"We'll find another way."

***

As the weather improved, the completion of the desk project left a void in their days. It had given shape and purpose to the winter. With more opportunities to get outside, Tim also began to grow restless with his schoolwork. As his reading and arithmetic assignments grew stale, Doug looked to diversify the curriculum. He began to build what he thought of as a music appreciation class. There were no instruments for them to play, but they could certainly listen. Now that the sun had intermittently returned, the solar panel received a more reliable daily charge. He felt safer using his phone, rather than feeling a need to reserve its battery for any contingency. They had managed so far without needing to flee with it at a moment's notice, even as the emergency bag stood ready by the door. So he began selecting short, accessible pieces of classical music from his phone's collection, one per week, for Tim to experience. He found that if the boy used headphones and listened to the music in private, in his workspace, he treated the undertaking more seriously and was less prone to tune out or wander away. He preferred this over listening together. The pieces had to be short and immediately engaging. Doug was no performer, but he did love music and had a good library of recordings. He tried to select a variety of styles and eras. Aaron Copland's "Fanfare for the Common Man." The aria to Bach's Goldberg Variations. The opening movement of Beethoven's Fifth Symphony. Erik Satie's Gymnopédies. The assignment was for Tim to listen to the piece three times per week and write down three new observations on each listen, for a total of nine. What instruments he heard. How the music made him feel. Whether it was fast or slow, loud or soft. If it made him think of a certain color, or a certain place. If he liked or disliked it, and if so, why.

With such innovations, they limped along toward a spring that seemed perennially out of reach. Doug found that he could generally fight inertia enough to stay a few steps ahead of surrender, even as it grasped and snatched at his heels. They never had a day where they simply gave up—on schooling, or cooking, or their life-sustaining routines. They always got dressed and they always made meals and they always left the kitchen tidy before going to sleep. Tim kept up his promise and ate the food placed in front of him, occasionally with a grimace. The remaining cans stood lonesome on the pantry shelf. Some days, it was hard to preserve any momentum. Occasionally he felt himself limping to the finish line of his bed. But they kept breathing and walking and moving forward through an endless and indeterminate pause in their regular lives. Yet he tried to remind himself: this isn't a pause in your life or some lost year. This is a year of your life. Nothing more or less. One of many. Perhaps its most vivid year. There would be—had already been—years of grief. Years of sickness. Years of worry. Fat years and lean ones. This was a year of hiding. A year of war. A year of safekeeping, above the fire. Many evenings, he thought that he would look back on how he had comported himself during this extraordinary time. He knew he was being tested. Not by God or the angry fates but by a capricious and unfair world and the shortsighted people who filled it. He wanted to pass the test. One day he wanted to look back with pride on how he had conducted himself. So far he had not exploded at his son, or fallen apart in his duties as the child's guardian. As much as he sometimes wished to curl up and will the world away, he had not done so. He thought he had made good decisions, based on the information he had at the time, to keep the two of them safe. He would only know later.

He began to perceive in himself a worrying inclination toward solitude. This did not apply to his son's company, which he relished. Instead, he shrank at the prospect of rejoining society. He feared he was losing the habit of existing among people in groups. It had never been the easiest thing for him in the best of times. The thought of a meeting room packed with adults filled him with dread. Their imagined voices and laughter made him wince. The awful noise of it, and the freewheeling unpredictability. All that sour breath. Too many opinions. Too much motion. He imagined situating himself by the door. And then stepping out for the restroom. Leaving prematurely and retreating to his office. Fearing an inquiry from a well-wishing colleague, he would leave the building for a walk. He would take his things just in case he ended up catching the train home. But the walk would take him onto crowded city streets. He would need to find a park. To move farther and farther away from everyone. And find himself where?

***

"What did you think of this one?" he asked after Tim listened to "Rejoice, O Virgin," by Sergei Rachmaninov for the first time. It was the sixth and culminating hymn in the great Russian composer's *Vespers*, an unaccompanied choral work to be sung as an evening vigil. The music had great personal significance for Doug, and he had hesitated to share it with his son in the event he did not like it or take it seriously. It was unbearably beautiful, a work in constant yet gentle motion, and its overtones resonated in the intervals of the Almighty. He had listened to this recording for decades and had heard the work performed live once, on the spur of the moment at a concert in New York many years earlier.

Sensing his father's vulnerability, the boy responded with a sensitivity he would not have displayed a year earlier. "I really liked it. It was different from the others. There were no instruments in this one, right? Just the singers?"

"That's right."

"Didn't grandma sing in a choir?"

"She sure did."

"Did she ever sing this song?"

"We'll have to ask her. What else did you notice?"

"I didn't know the words."

"They were singing in a different language, weren't they?"

"What language was it?"

"It's Russian."

"It sounded like church. It echoed. When they would stop singing, you could still hear it right afterward."

"That's a good observation. Three good ones, in fact: it echoed, a different language, and no instruments. I think you should write those down. What else did you notice?"

The boy thought for a moment. "I think I've heard it before."

"That might be. I might have played it around this house."

"It sounds like winter music."

"I agree."

"Soon it will be time for spring music."

***

April. They began a spring cleaning, airing out the cabin and scrubbing their living space with more energy and attention than they had paid it before. It was early in the season, and they likely had at least one more snow in their future. But on days when the temperature approached forty degrees with sunshine, it became impossible to keep still or stay inside. They threw open the doors and windows, brought the rugs out and beat them with broom handles, watered and scrubbed the muddy steps leading down from the front entry, and even addressed the frozen outhouses. They both enjoyed the feeling of motion in their limbs after their own hibernation.

When the sun set behind the mountains, it remained well below twenty degrees overnight, and they began to long for better food. Soon they would run out completely. The absence of coffee caused Doug numbing headaches that began in late morning and tightened to the point of intolerability by evening. Tim, at first game to make good on his promise, began to complain about the options that remained. Then he began leaving his plate half full after eating a few small bites. Then he started to lose weight. At night, Doug lay awake considering how they would even go about retrieving food from the observatory if they decided to try. He did not know if it was possible to get there. The snowpack had dwindled with each warm afternoon, but it continued to refreeze each night, making its retreat from the high altitudes in increments. What remained was rotten snow, icy and brittle as frosted spiderwebs. Hiking through it for mile upon mile in cold weather would be slow, dangerous work. Yet it needn't be the work of a single day. They could begin making their afternoon walks along the southbound traverse trail, breaking ground and assessing conditions. In this way they could gain a better understanding of the route and its feasibility. They did not have to come within sight of the observatory to have some sense of whether it could be reached. One evening, after a particularly contentious dinner with Tim refusing to eat much at all, he decided at least to do that much. Then he rolled over, tried to ignore his headache, and slept.

They started the next day and made it farther than he would have guessed. He brought the pike that they no longer needed for smashing up stream ice, using its pointed edge to break trail

where the path was unmanageable. It was clear no one had attempted to hike the traverse in months. The meandering lines
of frozen snowdrifts snaked along like ridgeline serpents. The
snow lay pockmarked and dirty in places, pebbled with earth and
riven by streams of snowmelt. Doug was impatient to see how
far they could proceed, but after they passed Mount Adams and
approached Mount Jefferson, he yielded to his son's request that
they turn around for the day. As far as the boy knew, they were
just having their afternoon walk. Not taking reconnaissance.

The following day they proceeded farther, and the next day
farther still, aided by good weather and unburdened by the need
to break trail for the first few miles. As they circled the flanks
of Mount Jefferson toward its south face, looking onto Mount
Washington, Doug decided to climb a hundred yards up a dry
aspect to a cluster of boulders to get a better look at the observatory through binoculars. It would be a trip of just fifteen
minutes. Tim decided to stay behind. They would remain in
sight of each other.

"I know, I know: if anything happens, blow the whistle,"
the boy said to his father.

"Actually, we won't do that today."

"Why not?"

"Well, I don't think it's a good idea to blow the whistle so
close to Mount Washington. We don't know if anyone is there
or might hear it."

"Oh."

"So we won't do that."

"What do I do if a bear comes?"

"I don't think we'll see any bears this high. There's nothing for bears to eat up here. But if there's danger, or you feel

unsafe, here's what to do. If you see a bear, you make your way up toward me. I'm going to be able to see you the whole time, and I'll look down and check on you every few minutes. If you see a person, hide behind those rocks right over there."

The boy looked alarmed. "Hide?"

"Just like when we play hide-and-seek. Hide there and keep quiet and still. And I'll be at your side before you know it."

He seemed unsure. "OK."

"You want to come up with me after all?"

"Yeah, I'll just come with you. How high are we going?"

From their perch above the trail, they had a clear view of the observatory. They could also see the network of paths that converged in the saddle between the two mountain peaks. They looked from the slope of Mount Jefferson, on which they stood, over the saddle below them and up to the summit of Mount Washington. The two peaks were situated close together, and the distance felt remarkably small even in the vast expanse. Their cluster of rocks offered good shelter from both the trail below and the observatory above them to the south. As they approached it, they saw that they could proceed up and around and into a sort of hollow of boulders, which were softened by lichen. Here the wind could not penetrate, and they could remain unseen from any direction but the summit of Mount Jefferson above and behind them, to the north. There was room enough to set down their things and lean back against the rocks for a rest. Sunshine had melted the snow. Doug helped the boy settle in comfortably with a snack before lying flat on his belly on the foremost boulder with his binoculars to see what he had come to see.

First the hollow between the mountains, and then the observatory: he scanned with careful deliberation. There was no one and nothing. The binoculars were of a good quality with long, wide lenses. They were no opera glasses. Following each trail as it crossed in and out of a central point marked by wooden signposts, he saw no hikers. Most of the snow had melted in the saddle and on the small rise of Mount Clay to the southeast. He followed the main trail as it switchbacked up to the summit and spotted no movement or bright color. On the flat peak of the great mountain, it was not possible to see every structure, but he slowly looked over what was in view. There was no one there. No smoke or steam rose from the building's exhaust vents. Although it was warm enough that he would not necessarily see this. No conspicuous gear or equipment lay outside that had not been there months before. He took out his field notepad and made a pencil sketch of the windows to record which blinds were open and which closed, not trusting his phone's camera to capture the image from so far away. He tried to record other indications of habitation that might change before the next scouting visit.

"Do you have your watch?" he asked Tim without turning around. "The one David gave you?"

"Yep."

"Set that timer on it for ten minutes, OK?"

"Why?"

"I'm going to look at the observatory for ten minutes to see if anything moves."

"OK, hang on a second." He fumbled through his pockets and carefully brought out the chronograph, manipulating the small chrome pushers that flanked its crown. He took his role in the endeavor seriously, inheriting the mantle of the watch's previous owner. "Starting . . . now."

The time elapsed with no movement or change. Wind whistled above and around their little nest and through the saddle between the two mountain peaks. Doug's hands began to grow numb, but he forced himself to maintain a frozen posture as though their safety depended on his stillness. In fact, it might. He realized that as he had taken one step and then another toward scouting out the observatory, he had all but committed to entering it and gathering food. He had hiked toward it, and then a bit closer, always carrying his rifle, and now here he was, within view of the objective and gaming out scenarios for when to move on it. He urged himself not to decide. Not yet. The next scouting trip should occur at twilight so they could see whether any lights came on in the evening. Although that would mean hiking back home in the dark. Or camping out in their enclave. At any rate, on the next trip, he could see whether any of the window shades had changed. They would wait a few days. This would give him time to cool on the plan if he needed to, and time to think.

"Ten minutes . . . now!" Tim said. He had been checking the watch regularly and closely monitoring it for the past four minutes. He enjoyed the smooth, even sweep of its mechanical second hand, so unlike the blocky, even *ticks* of the clocks he was used to on walls. The watch had become important to him, one of the few mementos of his mountain year, along with his spaceship, toy race car from Christmas, and of course his desk and chair. It remained much too big for his wrist, so he did not wear it. For that, he had his own child's size quartz wristwatch. But he wound David's chronograph every day and kept it on his desk. He brought it with him on excursions. Doug had been looking for an opportunity to have him use it.

"I like this place. This big rock and the other boulders near it," he said to the boy, as he sat down beside him and began eating peanuts.

"Me too. It's not as windy in here. It's like a fort."

"We should think of a name for it."

"Ooh! What about Tim's Rock?"

"Perfect name. That's what we'll call it."

"Can we come back here sometime?"

"You bet, buddy."

***

They saw a black bear on the way back to the cabin. Tim spotted it first: a sow with two cubs in tow, the size of jellybeans, four hundred yards below them in a field between stands of trees. The animals were down a steep rockfall from the two hikers and offered no possible threat. The man and boy stopped to watch through binoculars and riflescope as the mother led her cubs through the field at an ambling pace. The little ones' gaits were long-limbed and playful while their mother moved along in a husky pigeon-toed shuffle. They did not appear to have seen the humans, and Doug thought they must be too far away for scent. They must be avoided, and it was good to know that they were up from hibernation. Other bears would be about as well. But there was no threat today. He doubted they would seek flora or fauna as high up as the Presidential Traverse, where there was nothing at all to eat. Yet they must exercise even more caution around the Madison Spring campus by keeping the pantry closed and food put away and getting out of their bad winter habits of leaving dirty dishes on the table for an hour and more after mealtime.

As the afternoon waned, they walked home into dusk. The air grew colder. Blue light enveloped the mountain range, and their breath clouded the air before their faces. They walked, now astride, now in single file, as the trail conditions warranted. All around them, peaks comprised a darker midnight against the deepening hue of the sky. There was little sound but the crunch of their boots on snow. Doug shifted the rifle and moved it to his other shoulder. They walked in silence, tired from more exertion than usual and lost in their own forms of reverie. The boy played out his fantasies of action heroes and kung fu. His father thought about how to supply them for another season without unnecessary risk. When they rounded the final curve of Mount Adams and came into view of their little campus, its hut cast an inviting light against the darkness. As they descended into camp, Doug thought he heard something and stopped to look behind them and listen. But there was nothing.

***

Although Tim was initially keen to return to his fort, the idea of hiking the distance again daunted him and he demurred at the notion of another trip. Doug decided not to press the issue. He would use the pause to test his own belief in the plan. He needed some way to acquire perspective on weighing its risks versus rewards. In the meantime, his son continued to show little interest in the food available to him. He himself slept poorly.

In the night, as he lay staring at the ceiling, Doug sensed that the boy was also awake.

"Having trouble sleeping, pal?"

"Yeah."

"Everything OK?"

"Well, I was just wondering. Why did you want to look at Mount Washington for exactly ten minutes?"

Doug told him about the food.

"So you mean we'd be able to have pancakes again? And snickerdoodles? And grilled cheese?"

"Yes. We could have all those things again."

"Oooh, let's definitely do it!"

"Well, we have to see. I want to make sure nobody's there before I go inside. And Timmy: you couldn't come into the observatory with me."

"Why not?"

"Because it isn't safe."

"Where would I go?"

"You'd wait for me at Tim's Rock."

"By myself?"

"By yourself."

"But what if something happens to you?"

"Nothing's going to happen to me."

"But what if something does?"

"I'm not going to go in there until we're sure nothing will happen to me."

They both lay and said nothing.

"We'll make a plan, using your watch. We'll have you wait at Tim's Rock for two hours. If I'm not back by then, you'll come back here and wait for me. Do you think you can do that?"

"OK," Tim said, sounding unsure.

"Because if you're not up to it, we won't do it. I know it's scary being by yourself."

"What would happen if I had to come back here alone?"

"You remember how we looked at maps for getting down the mountain to the ranger station, right? If I don't return after a few days to the cabin, you'd follow the path and go there for help. You'd dress warmly and follow the map we made and the signposts that we talked about. You remember?"

"I remember."

"Let's think about it for a few days. We don't need to decide anything right now." He thought about whether to tie the decision to the boy's refusal to eat but did not want to weigh him down with that burden. If something were to go wrong, he did not want Tim to carry any guilt over having been its author.

***

They made another scouting trip later that week and confirmed that nothing at the observatory had changed. The blinds were the same and there were no fresh tracks on the traverse or signs of activity visible through binoculars. They felt once more like the only two people anywhere high in the White Mountains.

It was an impossible decision. Doug tried to weigh the remote risk of a catastrophe at the observatory against the looming impossibility of staying at their hut without resupply. How to balance such contingencies? Perhaps his conservative approach to risk no longer applied in a world of force and survival. He did not know what to do. Very soon an empty pantry would starve them out. They would find food or they would leave. Perhaps prematurely—pushed into the unknown world with far greater dangers, food security least among them. He had no one to help him think through the merits of action against inaction. If Carol were here, they would talk it out and reach consensus together. He suspected that any dozen parents would split down the middle on the proper course to take. But, at bottom, he knew that wrestling with this decision was a type of playacting within his own consciousness. He had known what he would do from the moment he saw that the observatory was empty. They would go. Tomorrow.

SEVEN

They set out before noon in clear weather. Doug stuffed his backpack with supplies that could last them the night, if need be, including sleeping bags, the small first aid kit, flashlights, food, and water. They both dressed in ample layers. He tried to make it feel like another scouting trip, but the boy sensed the higher stakes of the venture and carried himself in a tense and wordless manner. They made their preparations with deliberation before leaving and ate little lunch. Doug brought the rifle and all the ammunition, chambering a round. Using a pretext to return inside the cabin just before they left, he placed within view the map down the mountain to the ranger's station, as well as a final saved box of Tim's favorite granola bars and a note that he had prepared. He kept a fire burning.

They said little on their hike. The child had proved irritable at his father's constant attempts at reassurance. At a certain point, Doug realized these were merely his efforts to reassure himself. Man and boy wanted this day behind them. They walked. There had been no snowfall since their first trip to the observatory a week earlier, and the path was worn with the familiar tread of their bootprints. There were no other tracks human or animal in the frozen snow. As they cleared Mount Adams, a vista emerged to the west across the valley where they had lately seen the bears. The field below was still covered in white, but the snowpack melted further each day, opening holes of black in the ground like portals into some other dimension. Their high trail narrowed, and it was precarious enough that, in an earlier lifetime, Doug would have feared for his son's safety. But now he watched the boy walk ahead of him with assurance. He carried himself with a rolling gait that anticipated each bend in the trail as he looked out before him. He had grown taller over this strange season. Taller and stronger.

The boy slowed his pace as they approached their destination. Sensing his reluctance, Doug moved ahead and said he would lead for a while. When they reached the turnoff point, they both hiked up to the familiar spot together. The weather was fair, and temperatures were cool but not cold with the sun just past its zenith. The hollow provided cover from the wind. He settled Tim and showed him the supplies at hand. Turning away, he removed the folded duffel bag from his backpack and readied a few other items. The thinnest gloves would answer. He stowed his puffy jacket. He would move fast and light. Extra ammunition filled his pockets, ready to hand. The boy watched all this.

"Hop in your sleeping bag if you get chilly. Think of it like a blanket. It's not just for night times. Here's the phone. Don't use it for movies today; I just want you to have it in case. The charger is in the backpack. You've got your watch?"

Tim held it up. He had been clutching it inside his pocket like a totem. A small thumbprint blurred its crystal. This comfortable upper-middle-class boy drowning in possessions was now reduced to a single talisman measuring time. Which, in the end, was all he had. All anyone had. His father felt nearly unmanned by this unspeakable leave-taking. He decided it was best for both of them if he remained brisk and accomplished their business quickly.

"It's almost two o'clock. Stay here until four o'clock. Here are the extra binoculars. You can watch me, and I'll turn back and look at you every now and then. Thumbs-up means all good, flat palm means keep waiting, fist means hide here out of sight, circling finger means go to the cabin. Here, I wrote that down for you on this piece of paper. If I'm not back or in sight by four o'clock, you take the trail back home. Don't wait past four, and don't come to the observatory unless I'm there waving you to me, like this. If it's four, go home quickly and you'll get back before it's dark. Remember everything we talked about."

"I remember." The boy could barely meet his father's gaze. He was trying not to cry.

"Courage, my son. I'll be back soon." He cupped the boy's head in his hand and kissed him. "I love you."

"I love you."

He left at speed.

***

As he moved through the saddle and up the slope of Mount Washington, he worked himself into the cadence of a runner. In the thin air, his breathing became the soundtrack to his thoughts. At first his tears blinded him. Then his mind tried to wander to remonstrance: about the folly of this choice, or the time of day he had selected, or the supplies he had brought. He pushed the doubts away by trying to reconstruct the layout of the observatory. His son's worried face kept intruding. He read and reread the same paragraph of that awful departure. Surely, he would see his boy again.

He tried to visualize the observatory's layout. The door he would use was on the northwestern corner. They had walked through it at one point on the day they spent surveying the summit's plateau. It was not fifty feet from the storeroom he needed, on the lower floor. If that door was locked, he would use the one through which the hiking party had departed on that very early morning. On the main floor. He ran. He felt strong in his arms and legs, strong in his heart, strong in his lungs. Through these months of panic and tedium, doubt and survival, the mountains had filed him down to something essential, like the edge of a blade.

At intervals, he stopped and looked back through the binoculars to check on the boy. The first time, Tim was looking back at him through the field glasses of his own. At such a distance he was hard to keep within the confines of the lens. They exchanged the thumbs-up sign. The second time he was not in view at all. Doug thought his disappearance was progress. He must have crouched down into the hollow and made himself comfortable, settling in to wait. He turned back to the slope and scrambled over boulder and scree, working his way up the face. The trail's switchbacks extended the distance, and he skipped them altogether, going straight up rather than traversing from side to side. Time was what mattered now. Time during which his son was alone and he himself was exposed to view. As the trail steepened toward the peak, it became impossible to continue running, but he moved as quickly as he could, careful not to turn an ankle but determined not to slacken his pace. The observatory was no longer visible here directly below the top. As he prepared to summit, he decided to make for the same cairn of rocks marking the highest point of elevation where he and Tim had sheltered from the vortex so many months before.

Peering from behind it, he surveyed the mountaintop campus. Even this far into spring, it remained a picture of white Arctic rime. The fearsome winds that had coated every surface in horizontal frost must have been awesome indeed. Yet now all was still and empty. He saw the same white weather tower whose prominence marked the highest point in New England. Steel guylines anchored it to the mountain. There was the same turret-like corner of the observatory jutting out higher than the rest of the structure. A large snowcat vehicle was parked in the same place and covered in ice. Nothing about the summit had changed to his eye. He could not see to the eastern or southern aspects of the summit from here and briefly considered circling the observatory before going in. But he wanted to remain in view for Tim and decided it was best not to delay. He watched and waited a few moments longer, taking a drink from his water bottle and stuffing half of one of their last energy bars into his mouth. As he chewed, he let his heart slow down and his breathing settle. Removing his binoculars, he glassed the opposing mountain he had just left and had trouble at first locating Tim's Rock from such a distance. It was much farther down than he initially looked. But then he saw the distinctive cluster of boulders, no larger than pebbles, and studied it. Boulders of mighty tonnage laid there by unspeakable forces. A flood or a rockslide or the shifting of the very plates of the Earth. He could not see Tim. The only sound he heard was wind.

He turned and faced the observatory. The pair of doors he wanted was in sight and he ran toward it. Each door was gray steel with a square window crossed by the threaded lines of safety glass. The handles came together at sharp right angles. He peered through and saw only darkness. The door was unlocked, and he carefully pulled it open and felt the air inside escape. He checked his watch. The time read 2:37. He unshouldered his rifle and carried it in both hands as he stepped through very slowly. He took care to shut the door behind him silently. It did not latch. He stood still and listened.

***

What first struck him was the smell. He had stepped across a threshold into a dangerous receptacle of air and habitation. And now the recycled product of that building's vents and ducts enfolded him like the stale rush of an airplane's cabin. The air tasted repurposed to his nose after so much time in the fresh alpine. There was also an unpleasant tang, an odor, the pungent or even slightly rancid note of something gone off. Bad food or something in decay. It was an unfamiliar smell and it turned Doug's stomach. To the eye, the observatory looked much the same as before, neat and orderly with its linoleum floors and supply cabinets. Perhaps there were one or two additional signs of the passage of time. An opened drawer here, an out-of-place tray there. The floor did not shine as it had before. But there were no broken light fixtures dangling from the ceiling or garbage strewn about. It was not the scene of an unraveling.

The back corridor he had entered was one floor below the observatory's main level, which contained the cafeteria, tourist exhibits, and room where they had bivouacked. He needn't ascend to that floor to fulfill his purpose. The food storage he wanted was just around a corner on the eastern side of the observatory. He waited another minute and listened to make sure there were no sounds. Slowly, he dropped to his belly to begin crawling the distance. The sensors for the hallway's automatic lights were at a height of four feet. He had no notion of their sensitivity or whether the generators here still worked and supposed he might be able to walk very slowly and thereby avoid triggering the lights. But that would sacrifice time and add risk. It was better to stay low. He checked the rifle's safety once more and began his approach. For the return trip down the hallway, he planned to lie on his back, clutch the rifle and duffel to his chest, and push himself forward with his feet along the ground. He feared the clang of metal against the floor above all things.

As he made his way, he looked and listened. There was nothing. It felt for all the world as though he was inching along an abandoned hospital corridor. There was only one door between his entrance and his destination, and it was closed. A janitor's closet. He noticed a clock on the wall above him that had stopped running. No one had changed its battery. Dust balls and cobwebs had begun to accumulate along the wall's baseboards, which had not been cleaned in months. He marveled at his strange vantage. Half a year away from civilization and now his return to it came at an ant's eye view. At last he drew even with the pantry. Its door was open. As he entered, he breathed a sigh of relief to see abundant food of every description. Canned goods, pastas, snacks, staples, drinks, desserts. The industrial walk-in refrigerator and freezer were likewise provisioned to feed dozens of people for months. He scanned quickly and made brisk decisions about which items to replenish from their own exhausted stores and which to add anew. He smiled to see boxes of granola bars and bags of ground coffee. A critical few minutes went to searching for spices, which finally yielded cinnamon. They could bake their cookies again. Setting out the duffel bag, he packed carefully and systematically and, above all, quietly. He could carry enough food to last them through summer if they chose to stay that long. A second winter would require further resupply. He scanned the room to see if there was anything else that could be put to use. After a moment's consideration, he took a small hand crank radio that could pick up an emergency bulletin and charge a phone even in the absence of a working electrical socket. Then he checked the hallway, lay flat on his back, and looked toward the door through which he had entered. The lights remained off.

***

As he prepared to leave, another door twenty paces beyond the supply room caught his attention. The smell seemed to come from there. It looked like another supply room. The time was 2:54. He decided to make a quick pass for anything useful. He would also investigate the odor. He carefully set down the duffel and backpack just outside the supply room door and crawled toward the far door, in the other direction from his exit. As he approached it, the unpleasant smell grew stronger. It reminded him of the dead mouse they had aired out from their cabin's dormitory. He began to feel lightheaded, but curiosity mingled with his dread, and he felt he must see what lay around the corner. As he drew close, the stench became overpowering, like sweet and sour pork left for weeks in the sun.

He rounded the corner, and a mound of rotting food waste came into view. Everything from discarded wrappers to chicken bones to half-full dairy cartons lay strewn on the floor like some domestic landfill. Maggots had bloomed in the space and crowded over a glistening piece of bone and gristle. It looked as though someone had made a habit of casually tossing garbage in through the door while passing by. The smell flooded upon him, and he felt a sudden urge to retch. He covered his nose and mouth with his hand and backed away quickly.

As he did so he heard the muffled tread of footsteps coming from the floor above. He froze. Even in his disgust he did not think he had made a sound. He listened closely. There was only one person walking. Walking: not running. At a casual pace. It was not someone racing down the stairs to confront him. He thought his presence remained undetected. But he had stayed too long, and it was time to go. He was not alone in the observatory, as he had thought. He crawled to the room's door and crouched behind it, out of sight from the hallway. His rifle was in his hands, but he had left the duffel and his backpack in the hall. If anyone saw these things, they would know someone was here. He waited and listened. The footsteps above him moved again, seemingly back the way they had come. Like someone crossing a room to get a glass of water and then returning to his chair. He acted quickly. Crawling toward the exit door, he made his way through the hallway. In the event he would have to run, he decided to don the backpack and strap the duffel to his front before opening the outer door. He leaned his rifle against the wall next to the door and struggled into his luggage. Working with hasty imprecision, he pulled and struggled the backpack and then the duffel into place.

"What you got there?" said a voice behind him.

Doug dropped the duffel, grabbed his rifle, and spun around, pointing it at the chest of the man in the orange socks.

He was fifteen feet away. They faced each other. He did not appear to have a weapon. Doug studied him, this phantom of his mountaintop nightmares. The change to his appearance was shocking. His hair and beard were wild, and he had lost at least thirty pounds. He wore different clothes. In some places, they had disintegrated into tatters. Smears of grime covered the fronts of his pant legs. He wore clog-like house shoes of a strange description, as ill-fitting and bizarre as the rest of his costume.

"Why is it every time I see you, I feel like you're about a minute from killing me?" the man said to Doug.

"Are you armed?" Doug asked.

"What a question!"

"I'd like to know."

"I'm not." The man looked slightly amused. "What brings you here?"

"I just need food." He gestured toward the bag.

"Run out at your hut?"

"Almost."

"Well, there's plenty. Take what you need."

This was unexpected.

"You've got one bag there, but you might want two. Although I guess that's heavy. Most of the stuff in that pantry I don't touch. I've turned into more of a salami-and-crackers guy lately." He smiled. His smile was less menacing than Doug had remembered. He had aged terribly.

"I'm sorry about the gun," said Doug, slightly lowering his rifle but keeping both hands on it. "You startled me. I didn't think there was anybody else here."

"I told you I was living here."

"That was a long time ago. I thought you might have left."

"No plans to."

They looked at each other. The man did not seem desperate here on his home turf. Not formidable. Or perhaps Doug felt less defensive without Tim nearby to protect.

Doug lowered his rifle to his side. The last time they met, the man had seemed bewildered. Now he carried himself with greater assurance but no bravado. He had nothing to prove. Doug realized that he probably liked living here by himself.

"You've wintered here?"

"I have. It's been very cold. The wind on this summit is unreal."

"Any visitors?"

"Not a one. You?"

"Nobody at all."

"You and your kid managed alright? Heat and so forth?"

"Yes. The fire at Madison Spring has kept us warm."

"That's good to hear. There's propane here, as well, if you cook with that. Help yourself."

"Thanks. Just the food will do. What about news—any of that?"

"Stopped looking for it."

Doug started. "You mean you're not checking for signals?"

"I most certainly am not. New Year's resolution."

It took a moment for this to sink in. Four months. "But you've got the best communications in the whole national forest up here. If anybody can get Wi-Fi or cellular it's you. There might be peace down there and you'd never know!"

The man looked at Doug, and his eyes softened. The unnerving brashness that had characterized his earlier pronouncements was replaced by a hint of shame. Finally, he turned away and said quietly, "The truth is, I don't really want to go back down."

Doug waited for him to continue.

"I've been on my own most of my life. I doubt you know what that's like. You've got your son, I'm sure you've got a wife."

Doug said nothing.

"For a long time, that's what I wanted most. A family. Children. I tried my best to meet others. Make friends. Somehow none of that ever worked out for me."

"And now?"

"Now I finally found a place where it doesn't matter. I don't have to try. I don't have to watch everybody else enjoy the one thing I can't get. Instead, I've got fresh air. Clean water. And I've got the world's best view, right out my front door. Watch the prettiest sunrise every morning."

Doug listened.

"I'd rather stay here by myself. Self-reliance. That's Emerson. You ever read Emerson?"

"A little bit."

"If you'd read Emerson, you'd remember. Government's ruined everything down there anyway," he said with a flash of his former heat. But this time it was not pointed at anyone.

"And when all this is finally over, what then?"

"Oh, I don't know. Not many years left on me. If they come and force me out, I might just set off into the mountains and not come back."

"Isn't it lonely?"

The man gazed at Doug as though he had not been listening. "No lonelier than it's ever been."

***

They walked home in silence. After learning of the encounter and seeing his father's mood, Tim understood that they were safe and had gotten what they needed. An hour into their hike, they reached a lookout, and Doug turned with the binoculars and glassed the trail for several miles behind them. Mount Washington was no longer in view, eclipsed now by Mount Jefferson. For a time, the man in the orange socks had watched them like a sentinel guarding a ruin. Their familiar northbound trail bore them home as the shadows lengthened in the late afternoon. They gazed over the valley to the west. Doug looked about him and saw the landscape with fresh eyes. He tried to imagine the perspective of a man who would renounce society and adopt this country permanently. The late-spring snow bowing the branches of the pines. Roots and rocks fighting for prominence on the narrow path. Spindrift blowing off the summits in the vertiginous manner of alpine clouds. The sharp point of Mount Madison, rearing up ahead. It was all so beautiful yet desperately empty. He suddenly longed for human connection. A handshake. An embrace. An exchange of laughter. That man had none of those things. Doug no longer feared harm at his hands. Instead, he began to fear the man's withdrawal into a hermetic life. Eventually it would become easier to drift into that mindset than to return to what had come before.

Later on during their hike, as Doug gazed westward across the valley, he perceived an extraordinary sight in the direction of Littleton. In the fading afternoon, he thought he saw the glow of electric lights. He said nothing to his son but watched with great intensity as he walked. Once or twice, he stumbled and had to return his attention to his footing. When he looked up again, the light was gone. Perhaps the power had been restored. Or maybe the process of restoring it had finally begun. He would check for Wi-Fi and cellular signals as soon as they returned to their cabin. When they navigated around the last bend of Mount Adams, their campus came into view in its sheltered hollow. The yellow light from the windows cast by their fire beckoned them home. Spent adrenaline leeched out of him and he wanted nothing more than to go in and lie down and sleep. First he took care to remove the map and other things he had placed out for the boy as a contingency. He checked and there were still no Wi-Fi or cellular signals. The power was not yet restored, although the flicker prefigured its return one day soon.

They celebrated their replenished larder with a dinner of hot cocoa and popcorn. Doug had no energy to prepare more than that. They ate in muted celebration after so much fatigue and stress. Their cabin was inviting and provided a warm domestic contrast with the disordered observatory. As they made their preparations for bed, he felt the blaze of the hearth reach his aching bones. He removed hearthstones from their beds, which warmed the frostbitten space where their feet would lie in the bedclothes. Before sleep came, Tim spoke from his bed. His father realized he had neglected to invite the boy to process the events of the day. If Carol were here, she would have done so first thing. They faced each other, propped on elbows.

"Dad?"

"Yeah, pal?"

"Did the man in the orange socks have a gun too?"

"No. At least, I didn't see one."

"Were you scared when you were talking to him today?"

"I was startled at first. And I didn't really want to see him. But after a while I realized I didn't need to be scared of him."

"Why not?"

"He was friendlier this time."

"Did you ask him if he wanted to come live with us?"

"No, my guy."

"I'm glad."

"Yeah?"

"Yeah. I think it's better just us. Nobody else."

Doug studied his son's face in the firelight.

"But I wonder if he was lonely," the boy continued.

"I think he was very lonely."

"Do you think he would have wanted to come live with us?"

"No, I don't think so."

"Even though he was lonely?"

"I think he's gotten used to being lonely. I think he's so used to it that that's what he prefers now."

"Like how we're used to living in the mountains?"

"A bit like that."

"I'm glad we live here now."

"You are?"

"Yeah. I think it's better here."

"Why?"

"I don't have to go to school, and there's no annoying rules I have to follow or mean teachers, or anything like that."

Doug looked at his son and made a decision. This time it would be his own, whether or not he was ready.

"Well, don't get *too* used to it," he said.

"What do you mean?"

"Because we'll be leaving when it gets warmer."

"Leaving the cabin?"

"Yes."

"Going back to our house?"

"That's right."

"When?"

"When more of the snow melts." Tim said nothing, so his father asked, "How does that sound?"

The boy thought quietly for a moment. He said: "I'll be sad to leave, but I think I want to go."

***

The decision changed the tone of the cabin from the next dawn. It ceased to feel like home and instead took on the aspect of a seasonal retreat. A clock now ticked down toward their departure. The four walls no longer belonged to them. Doug began to imagine other people who had stayed there before, and others who would visit in the future. They found themselves talking about what it would be like to revisit familiar rooms in their Boston house, or landmarks in their neighborhood, or especially to see people they had missed. In lighter moods, they tormented each other by naming favorite foods they had done without, which they might soon enjoy once more. Chocolate ice cream. Pizza. Indian takeout. A Happy Meal. The thought of an imminent return to their former life, so close within reach and yet for the moment out of grasp, gave them a hope they could not yet believe in. Would it still exist? How would it differ? Would something stand in their way? Could they bear to wait now that the decision had been made? Yet waiting was all they could do. The season must progress, or they could not hike down. The snow in places remained higher than the boy's waist. Doug told himself not to wait too long: early May at the latest. He was stepping forward in deciding to act, and he must not put up roadblocks. As was his habit.

They began spending afternoons reordering the campus like visitors preparing to hand in their keys. Doug enlisted Tim in making an inventory of the storeroom, which included recopying the last scrawled page of supplies in a neater hand. The boy's penmanship had steadily improved through weeks of persistent exercises. They picked up on their spring cleaning. The dormitory needed airing and sweeping after being shut in for several weeks. The kitchen required attention as well, and they returned to their initial habit of reusing a single set of tableware each, carefully washed, rather than cycling through the entire supply and letting dishes pile up. Doug made a special project of ensuring that David's apartment was restored to the monastic order in which he had left it. Whether or not their friend ever came back to this place, he would want it maintained in a certain way. They reshelved the books they had borrowed. Doug proudly returned the bottle of Scotch, which yet contained a measure or two. Those few fingers of liquor were a testament to his discipline and represented disorder kept at bay. Each day, he checked for cellular and Wi-Fi signals and received no encouragement. Yet the sign of light he had seen was a beacon. Order was returning below, and they must seek it out. This would always entail a leap of faith.

Evenings and mornings were still cold enough to require a fire, but they let it burn out throughout the day. As May approached, the sunny afternoons gave them a chance to get outside and hike the environs. They took long walks for exercise and to survey the landscape. Once more, they visited the timberfall to collect firewood, this time to replenish what they had taken. Doug brought the rifle and kept alert for bears, but they saw none. They had their best conversations as they walked. Tim increasingly spoke of the future, and these conversations created a sort of momentum that carried them both through the late spring. Doug marveled at the way the boy had grown in this extraordinary season, from a clinging child into an adolescent capable of chatting about topics that ranged widely. He began to take an interest in astronomy, and they discussed their favorite planets, and those planets' moons. They planned ahead and dreamt aloud.

"I'm actually looking forward to going back to school," Tim said one day.

"You are?"

"Yeah."

"Which part are you looking forward to?"

"Seeing my friends. Playing at recess. Playing soccer in gym. Stuff like that."

"That sounds nice. Remember though, we don't know quite when school will start again. Hopefully this fall."

"Why?"

"Well, we don't know how things are down there yet."

"Are they safe?"

"That's what we're going to find out."

"If it's not safe, will we come back up here?"

"I'm not sure. We'll play it by ear. If it's not safe to go home yet, we might try to find David at his daughter's house. What else are you looking forward to?"

"Swimming this summer."

"That sounds fun. I'm looking forward to swimming too."

"Will the pool be open?"

"I don't know. But if it isn't, we can always swim in the ocean or a lake."

"That would be even better. We can pack the pool bag with chips and juice."

"And pickles."

"*Dad.*"

***

Snow receded from the campus even as the peaks above sparkled a brilliant white. On some days, they hiked the topmost section of the trail that they would use to depart. It would not be long now. At the highest reaches of the timberline, the snow remained well-established in the shade of the pines. But Doug suspected that it would disappear quickly as they shed elevation. Winter had yielded to spring even here. Thousands of feet below them, the air would be warm indeed. One afternoon, on such an excursion, Tim noticed a field that had shaken free of snow and emerged into a bloom of wildflowers. The sun illuminated painted trilliums and sheep laurels, which they both walked over to see. The hazy tinge of summer lay over the meadow in warm beams of light.

"You have very good eyes, Timmy. I would have walked right by these."

"So pretty," the boy said reverently as they stood among the blooms.

"You know, tomorrow is Mother's Day."

"It is?"

"Should we gather a few flowers and bring them up to the cabin?"

"No, I don't think so."

"No?"

"I think Mom would like them better here. This way maybe other people will see them too."

Doug watched the boy studying the flowers and touching the petals with his small fingertips.

"Dad?"

"Yeah?"

"What was the last thing Mom ever said to you?"

Birdsong filled the meadow as they stood together. "I'll tell you what one of the last things was." He took his son's hand, kissed it, and then held it. "She said, 'The thing I'll be sorriest to miss is seeing Tim be a father one day.'"

The boy looked at him in wonder. "She said that?"

"Mm-hmm." He smiled. "Because she knew you'd be so good at it."

Tim looked back at the flowers and smiled. "How much do you like being a dad?" he asked.

"I like it fifty and a million."

"And Mom always said that's the most."

"Mom was right."

***

On the morning of their departure, they packed the things they might need on the road. The phone's charger. The CB radio. Portable food. Rain gear. Medical supplies. The car keys, which thankfully remained clipped to the lanyard inside Doug's backpack. As he doused their last fire, he watched his son carefully pack his spaceship and Christmas race car toy. They dressed in layers and filled their pockets with food. He insisted that they both drink water, and they carried enough for several days. The great room looked small with the fire out and their possessions stripped away. They had not attempted to move the heavy beds back to the dormitory, and the desk and stool remained. But otherwise, the cabin was as they had found it. The guest book bore their signatures and the improbable dates of their visit. They stepped outside and faced the enormity of the mountains. Neither knew where they would next lay their heads. They stepped forward and abandoned their home. Now they had only each other.

They turned north and began to hike their way down Mount Madison. There were no tracks other than their own in the snow. No one had hiked in or out this way since the prior year. Soon they were enveloped in trees. Under the evergreen canopy, the air grew cool. The temperature shifted as suddenly as a cold patch in a summer lake. They walked close together and said little. It was the last march of their journey through these mountains. Their feet knew what to do, and they hardly exerted themselves with the work. Walking downhill was a rare treat. In time, the foliage thickened, and the snow grew thin, then sparse, then disappeared except in the shaded hollows that received no sunlight at all. The path was muddy from trickles of spring runoff. Its downward slope made easy going, even as the miles accumulated. Mud coated their boots, and their legs were strong. Doug reflected on how little had separated them from the world and all its complications during this most remarkable of seasons. A half dozen miles and five thousand vertical feet. While his body was at ease, his mind wandered. He hiked with more assurance than he felt, despite his confidence in the decision to leave. The sense of being untethered from any worldly place unsettled him. He felt like an astronaut suddenly floating free of all structures, hoping to bump into something solid and familiar.

When they broke through the canopy to the trailhead, he felt a strange instinct to crouch and find cover. The world could see them once more. But there was no need. The parking lot was nearly empty. By the look of it, no one had been there in quite some time. Their car sat where he had left it, the windshield covered in grime. When he tried to start it, the engine would not turn over. The battery had long since died. He was not entirely surprised. They gathered a few things from the trunk and then scanned the trailhead board for any news or notices. It contained topographical maps and familiar reminders about trail upkeep and packing out waste. A small blaze showed the Danish flag, and underneath it, a heart. Their friends had made a point of coming this way to leave one last sign of friendship. The artwork bore Linda's hallmark. Doug and Tim smiled as they recalled their friends from the prior year.

"What do we do now?" Tim asked.

"Now we walk to the ranger's station. The one on our map. Want to take a break first? It's about a mile from here."

"How long will that take?"

"Twenty minutes."

"Let's just keep going and then we can rest when we get there."

"Good idea."

***

They saw no people on the curving road. Overhead, a mild breeze rustled the spring leaves. The temperature here was at least fifteen degrees warmer than it had been at the cabin. There was much less wind. They both removed their jackets and walked in shirtsleeves. It was pleasant going, but they were tired and apprehensive about what came next. Doug had known that the car would likely be unavailable to them, but proceeding on foot limited their options. If he came across other cars, he could see if they had a portable battery jumper. But the only one they saw was a burned-out husk, with little left but the chassis. The sight of it filled them both with fear. The silence pulsed at another frequency than in the mountains. It was the difference between an empty room and the pause before someone speaks. Doug had brought the rifle with him, and it took an effort to keep it slung on his shoulder rather than close in his hands.

When they rounded the corner to the ranger's station, he had a memory of having seen it before. He would have driven past at the start of their hike the previous October. It was a small building, about the size of the Madison Spring Hut, with a stone fireplace and beige siding. There were no signs of any occupancy or staffing. The small adjacent parking lot was empty, and the chimney stood cold. The building's lights were off. The front and back doors were locked, but Doug found an unlatched side window and they gained entry in that way. He called out a greeting as they stepped inside but no one was there. They made a tour of the rooms. The front area contained a desk for customer interactions and office space stood behind. Upstairs were rooms for supply and storage.

Tim sat down to rest and eat a snack as his father made a closer inspection of what seemed to be the main office. Six months earlier, the boy would not have been separated from his parent at such a moment. The space remained organized and there were no indications of disorder or panic. He did see a large regional map with unaccountable tack marks on it that seemed to have been hastily placed on a wall: tracking signals of some variety. The very fact of the station's abandonment was its own commentary on the state of the continued crisis. If order had returned to the world, then someone would be here. And power would be restored. A fine layer of dust coated everything. As he walked past a desk, he drew his finger along its surface like a butler making his inspection. The window looked out to the street, where the road curved on ahead in the direction they had walked. He wondered when the last car had traveled this way. They would need a car if they were to get to Boston or Vermont.

Surveying a bulletin board, his eye wandered from duty schedules to fire season warnings that had been left up from the previous summer. He scanned the names of employees scheduled for shifts in the various backcountry huts and saw that David's last name was Sullivan. Such a conventional name for a mystic. His eyes wandered over the rest of the board for any information that might prove useful. Just before giving up, his glance came to rest on an envelope marked "D & T" tacked to the lower corner. Here was what he had hoped to see. On a folded sheet of paper inside, in a distinctive hand, was written, "*Dear Doug, If this note finds you, then you and Tim will have come down from the mountains. I'm back from Burlington. Sorry I wasn't able to wait for you. You'll find me in my home about twelve miles west of the ranger's station. Visit me and stay as long as you like. I hope to come up and check on you both this spring when the snow melts. I left two bicycles for you in the shed behind the station. The lock combination is 24-34-12. Here is a map to my house. Your friend, David.*" The note was dated in late January.

Tim was elated by the discovery and asked to keep the note. He read and reread it, fascinated by the old man's distinctive cursive. Its leaden whorls and swoops were set down in the hand of some earlier correspondent. The boy carefully added the document to his store of simple possessions. Doug quietly rejoiced at the old man's safety and felt a valve inside him releasing months of worry. He also felt a surge of optimism knowing that their departure from the mountains had not been a mistake. They checked the condition of the bicycles, which had more or less full tires, and decided to stay the night in the station before setting out the following morning. They had plenty to eat in their backpacks and replenished their stores from the boxes of energy bars in a closet in one of the offices. As evening drew near, Doug made sure the doors and windows to the station were locked. He decided it would be safest not to draw attention to their presence with candlelight. They were tired enough to settle in for bed as darkness arrived. With moonlight playing in through the window, they talked about David's letter and what it portended.

"I bet his house is cool. Do you think he has a trampoline?"

Doug laughed. "I'm not sure. He's pretty old to be bouncing on trampolines."

"But he said he had grandkids. Cool grandparents get stuff like that for when their grandkids come visit."

"That's a good point. I hadn't thought of that."

"You should do that when you're a grandpa."

"You think I'm that old? That I'm already thinking of what I'll do when I'm a grandpa?"

"Well, your beard is pretty white."

"Watch out, bucko, or I'll tickle you."

"You're too old to catch me."

They laughed as a sense of possibility filled the small room. Man and boy slept well without dreaming.

***

The bicycle journey to David's house was full of sunshine and hope. The bikes suited them well enough after a seat adjustment made Tim's workable for his height. He disliked its green color but otherwise had no complaints. Riding under heavy backpacks was cumbersome, but it did not matter. The feel of the wind on their faces reminded them of an earlier time. They had both loved riding down a hill near their house, which ended in a favorite park. They talked about it as they pedaled. The day had broken clear and fine.

David's route took them along back roads. A quick study

of the map showed that this had been a deliberate choice.
The more direct path would have used a state highway, but
this would render them conspicuous and be in any event
unsafe for cycling travelers. If there were any drivers. As
they moved through the New Hampshire countryside and
away from the mountains, they began to pass houses, which
were spread out from each other and separated from the
roads by long gravel driveways. It was early in the day, and
most of the houses were quiet. But there was one man out
drinking coffee on his porch. Doug raised an arm in greeting without slowing down his bike and the homesteader
returned his wave.

As they approached their destination, the houses remained spaced at a generous remove. Each stood a quarter
mile off from its neighbor. Every home encompassed a sig-
nificant piece of land, even if it was modest, scrubby forest.
They searched for David's house. Doug looked forward to
shaking hands with a man he had come to regard as an old
friend, though they had shared less than a day of fellowship.
They passed a house that seemed to be occupied and had a
litter of toys in the front yard: big wheels, scooters, frisbees,
and footballs. Tim noted these signs of life with interest but
said nothing and remained fixed on his goal. A mile or so
after this one, they saw a house set back farther from the
others. There was a Volkswagen bus parked out front, and
Doug knew at once they had reached David's home. It was
a simple ranch house that bore the hallmarks of its owner.
A unique sundial was placed by the front walkway, and
a row of Himalayan prayer flags was strung between two
trees. The house stood dark and was far enough away from

neighboring properties that they both slowed their bicycles in tandem to double-check the address. Doug called out but received no answer.

"Why don't you wait here a minute while I go in and check," he said to Tim.

"OK. But don't take too long."

"I won't. Want me to call out Marco Polo so you can hear where I am?"

"No, that's OK."

Doug smiled. "I won't be long. Let's get you a snack. That was a serious bike ride."

Tim watched as his father entered the front door and called David's name once more. Then he disappeared inside the house. The boy waited and looked around the yard. The grass was long. Dandelions had begun to bloom. He laid down his bike and began to pick a few. The yellow blossoms stained his fingertips with scent and color. He moved from one patch to another. Soon he checked his watch. It had been three minutes. He picked up another flower and made a silent wish, then blew. His father reappeared in the doorway, looking grave.

"Timmy? Stay outside a few more minutes."

"Is David there?" he called back.

"Stay put. I'll be back soon."

The boy watched as his father disappeared into the house again. He tried to understand the meaning of these events. It was very hard to be patient after so much waiting. A moment later he saw a window open. Then another.

***

They sat together on a rock in the yard. The sun warmed their shoulders and tanned their faces. Tim cried intermittently but had no notion of grieving properly. He knew only that one more thing had been taken away and that the pain was real.

"He died in his sleep. It was peaceful. It's the best way to die."

"How can there be a best way to die? Dying is awful!"

"Everybody dies eventually. And David was an old man who lived a long life. So it's sad but it's not *all* sad."

"When did he die?"

"I think probably three or four months ago."

"But why can't I see him? I want to say goodbye."

"No, sweetie. He's been gone too long. He doesn't look like himself anymore."

"I got to say goodbye to Mom."

"I know you did."

"It's not fair."

"It sure isn't."

***

That afternoon, they buried their friend under the shade of a white cedar. Birdsong accompanied their efforts. Doug gave himself over to work that required the use of his hands and shoulders, legs and back. He felt a connection to the labor he had performed at the timberfall. The garage had the necessary tools. Tim wanted to be included and he contributed as well, at times crying angrily as he swung a shovel into the dirt and loosened stones and earth. They dug and rested. When they had finished, they took a longer break. The boy said he wanted to be alone for a while. Doug entered the house to see if he could find something to read aloud at the graveside. He had no notion of the Eastern religions and did not think that scripture would be appropriate. His eyes scanned the titles. Among the books, he noticed a volume he had read years before. He flipped through its pages until he found the passage he remembered. He and his son completed the interment, carefully lowering David, wrapped in white, back to the place of corruption. They covered him with earth and Doug opened the book and read aloud.

"'Three thoughts carry me ahead; the prospect of the northward view from Dolpo to Tibet; the prospect of a free descent across these brilliant snowfields to hot tea and biscuits; and the perception—at this altitude, extremely moving—that these two hands I see before me in the sun, bracing the basket straps, hands square and brown and wrinkled with the scars of life, are no different from the old hands of my father. Simultaneously, I am myself, the child I was, the old man I will be.' David, we are glad to have known you. You helped us at an important time in our lives. You helped many travelers enjoy the mountains, which we know you loved. You were a father and a grandfather. I'm glad your life's journey ended here, in your own home. You were a good man. I hope you found peace." He turned to his son and took his hand. "Would you like to say something?"

Tim stood silently for a moment. Then he said in a small voice, "Thank you for teaching me how to bake cookies. And for giving me your watch. I promise to take care of it. Thank you for being my friend."

***

Doug awoke for the second morning in a row in a country home.
The twin bed's cotton sheets were softened with age, their pattern faded to a mere suggestion and their elastic almost spent. A
heavy quilt covered the bed. He inhaled his first waking breath
of the day and looked over to see his sleeping son. They usually woke within a few moments of each other. He would wait
for the boy before getting up and going to the kitchen. The
floorboards of David's house made creeping out of the room
impossible. They had been laid down in another time and had
supported many a footstep.

At the breakfast table, he kissed his boy and cradled his
head in his hands. His hair smelled of plain soap. They had
both taken long baths and explored the house fully. The room
they had come to occupy seemed to have once been a child's
bedroom and had later been repurposed for guests. Out of respect for their departed host, they kept David's bedroom door
closed. They enjoyed the amenities of a house closer to sea level.
There were different foods, and the mere ability to step outside
in short sleeves was a revelation. At one point in the day, the
power flickered on for a moment and then switched off again.
It was like the blinking he had seen at Littleton from their hike
some weeks earlier.

"Will we have to do school today?" Tim asked after he finished eating.

"Not today. I thought we'd go take a walk and see what the
area is like."

"Or maybe take the bikes?"

"Even better."

He struggled over whether to bring the rifle. He had never
once used it, but having it at hand had given him a sense of

security. If carrying it through an abandoned landscape had felt necessary, this was not the day to set it down. They were liable to encounter people for the first time in half a year. It seemed foolhardy to step out unprotected on this of all occasions. Yet something about the environs and the ritual they had just enacted made it seem right to put themselves forward in a posture of trust. David had been safe enough here to die peacefully in his bed and to go unnoticed for months afterward. Doug left the house with the door unlocked and his hands free at his sides.

They rode their bicycles once more. He knew where to begin, and they rode east, in the direction of the mountains. As he recalled, they would not have to go far. The boy set out in front and his father marveled at how easy he made things look. His gifts were manifold. So were their blessings. He was at least three inches taller than when all this had begun. His hair was darker, and his eyes reflected more of the world. As they passed one house and then another, their destination came into view. The front yard full of toys was just before the next hill. Tim understood where his father had pointed them and looked back with an excited smile. As they drew nearer, they both heard the sound of children's laughter.

———

In memory of my father

MARTIN JAMES O'DONNELL

1946–2023

———

ACKNOWLEDGMENTS

I would like to express my gratitude to a number of kind and talented individuals at Blackstone Publishing, starting with CEO Josh Stanton, President Anthony Goff, and COO Megan Bixler. I am indebted to senior publicist Sarah Bonamino, print editor Levi Coren, managing editor Ananda Finwall, designer Alenka Linaschke, marketing editor Azalea Micketti, and compositor Katrina Tan. Special thanks to senior acquisitions editor Addi Wright for bringing me on board and to editorial director Josie Woodbridge for showing me the ropes. Every writer should be so lucky as to find a publishing team as dedicated and professional as I have.

Three people deserve particular mention for this book's journey into print. Michael Signorelli has the keen eye and light touch of a truly great editor. He steered the manuscript many critical compass points closer to true north. In the process, he gained a fan and became a friend. Jim Mustich, who published some of my earliest journalism, has been a warm and supportive champion of my literary efforts for more than fifteen years. Through Jim, I met Paul Feldstein, my agent, who believed in this book from the moment he read it and worked tirelessly to see it published. Michael, Jim, and Paul: my gratitude to you knows no bounds.

On a personal note, I would like to tip my hat to my lifelong friend Adam Siegel. Together the two of us have hiked mountain trails all over the world, including the Presidential Traverse, which inspired the setting for this book. I have been fortunate beyond words over the years for the support and encouragement of my brother, Patrick O'Donnell, my sister, Kathleen Odinga, and my beloved parents, Kitty and Martin O'Donnell.

This book is dedicated to my son, James. My hope is that one day he will read it and recognize it as a love letter. Above all, I wish to say that every word I write comes from the inspiration, belief, and love of my wife, Mary, without whom, for me, nothing is possible.